I Want To Be That Dog.....

Table of Contents

I Want To Be That Dog....

By
Brett Shayler

Dedication

I dedicate this book to all search and rescue dogs whose loyalty and dedication exemplify the extraordinary human-animal bond. To the dogs who tirelessly sniff out hope in the darkest places, navigate treacherous terrains with unwavering focus, and offer comfort and solace in times of despair, this story is a tribute to your heroic hearts.

It honors the handlers who dedicate countless hours to training and working alongside these extraordinary animals. Your patience, compassion, and unwavering commitment are vital to every mission's success. You are the quiet strength behind the brave bark, the steady hand that guides the searching nose, the compassionate heart that understands the language of a dog's devotion. Your dedication is an inspiration.

This book also belongs to those who have experienced the devastating loss of a loved one, only to discover a glimmer of hope amid the despair through the tireless efforts of a search and rescue team. Your resilience, strength, and unwavering belief in the power of hope inspired this tale. Your stories testify to the enduring human spirit and remind us of the profound impact animals can have on our lives.

This dedication extends to countless pups, still in their early days and full of playful energy with curious noses. Perhaps this story ignites inspiration, hinting at the journey they could take, fueled by courage and trained with dedication, offering hope. May their futures be joyful and fulfilling as they serve others. May their tails wag with the pride of a life dedicated to service, proving that even the smallest paw can make the most significant difference. Thank you for your dedicated service. You should share and remember their stories.

I also wanted to mention that I will donate all royalties from the sale of this book to "The Compass Foundation," a 501(c)(3) organization that supports Search and Rescue teams.

CHAPTER 1
Three Months Old and Filled with Pups

The world exploded into a kaleidoscope of sensations as I opened my eyes. It was not a gentle awakening but a tidal wave of smells—sharp, sweet, earthy, and a wild, messy flood I wasn't ready for. My tiny nose twitched, striving to decode the chaotic symphony of scents. My mother's warm, milky scent lingered faintly at the edges of my awareness. Then, a new aroma emerged: soft, clean, and slightly floral—my human scent.

I stumbled forward, my paws unsteady yet eager, landing on a warm, soft surface that gently gave beneath my weight. Beneath me, a steady, rhythmic thump echoed, the soothing sound of a calm heartbeat. This was not the rough, uneven ground of the whelping box; it felt... different. Safe.

I explored tentatively, my tongue lolling out as I tasted the air, with a tiny, wet nose sniffing everything within reach. Everything felt new, and strangely magnetic—like the world was daring me to explore it. There were soft things–blankets, perhaps?—that smelled faintly of soap and sunshine. I nuzzled them, my tail thumping a hesitant rhythm against the surface. The sounds were just as strange, just as alive. The rhythmic thumping continued, now accompanied by a gentle murmur. A large, warm hand stroked my head; its touch was soft and reassuring. The voice calmed the swirling chaos of my senses, providing a soothing calm amid the storm of new experiences. I nestled closer, seeking the source of this comforting warmth and sound.

Days turned into weeks. My experiences began slowly but soon gathered momentum. The house transformed into a familiar maze, filled with comforting scents and sounds. The delightful aroma from the kitchen became an endless source of fascination. I followed my human everywhere, a fluffy shadow at their heels, my tail wagging uncontrollably with excitement.

Learning about the house was a journey of exploration and discovery. The living room became my favorite playground, with its plush carpet and toys scattered throughout. I chased after shimmering dust motes, pounced on unseen foes—mostly imaginary mice—and collapsed in exhausted contentment, sprawled across the soft rug. Sleep came quickly, punctuated by playful energy and an insatiable desire to explore. Of course, accidents were inevitable. My still-developing bladder frequently betrayed me. The resulting scoldings were confusing, a mix of sharp sounds and displeasing scents I could not comprehend. However, the comforting touch and gentle words that followed softened even these moments, reassuring me that my clumsy mistakes did not diminish the love I received.

My human's hands, initially strange and large, became a source of comfort and play. Gentle strokes along my back soothed my anxieties, and a firm but playful tug on my ear started tug-of-war games. I associated their presence with warmth, safety, and endless affection. They were my world, protector, and source of all good things.

The world outside the house was equally captivating. The backyard — a vast expanse of grass and trees — became my personal adventure playground. Each blade of grass was a thrilling discovery, its texture unique and its scent subtly different from every other blade. I couldn't get enough of the earthy and invigorating smell of freshly cut grass, which filled my nostrils like a heady perfume. The chirping of birds, the buzzing of bees, the rustling of leaves—a symphony of sounds that painted a vivid picture of the world around me. The feel of dirt beneath my paws, the smooth coolness of the patio stones, the roughness of the tree bark—each texture a new experience to be explored and understood.

My human's scent followed me through the house, clinging to their clothes, furniture, and even the air they breathed. It was a constant, comforting presence, a reassurance in the chaotic world of smells and sounds. I learned to distinguish their scent from others, a beacon in the vast ocean of olfactory experiences.

A new sound emerged one day—a series of repetitive clicks and whistles. At first, I was not sure what to make of it. But then, I saw my human's hand move, fingers pointing in a specific direction. The clicks and whistles were followed by soft and encouraging words: "Sit," "Stay," and "Come." They were teaching me, guiding me, and patiently helping me understand this new language.

The training sessions were an odd blend of frustration and progress. My attention span was still short, and staying focused often felt like a battle. My clumsy paws didn't always manage to follow the instructions just right. Sometimes, I would have preferred to chase a butterfly or explore a fascinating scent rather than focus on "sit" and "stay." But there was also a thrill in mastering the commands, an accomplishment that was rewarded when my human praised my efforts with happy words and joyful pats.

The bond between us strengthened with each passing day. It was not a relationship based on food and shelter; it was something more profound, built on mutual affection and understanding. I learned to interpret the nuances of their body language—the subtle shifts in posture, the tone of their voice, and the expressions in their eyes. They, in turn, began to understand my way of communicating—the wagging tail, the excited barks, the soulful gaze.

My world expanded to include other humans. A loving smile from my human's family members, the soft touch of a child's hand, the warmth of laughter echoing through the house – these experiences enriched my life, adding layers of love and connection. I was surrounded by caring people who played with me, taught me, and showed affection. My days were full of games, naps, and love.

The days were not all perfect, of course. There were minor accidents, frustrating moments during training, and occasional puppy-related mischief. But the mistakes only reinforced the love and support I received from my human family, creating a stronger and more loving bond between us.

The support I received made minor challenges seem unimportant. I had found my pack, and my place was steadied by something I didn't yet have words for. This was home. This was my life. And it was glorious.

CHAPTER 2
Discovering My Human

The sharp and enticing scent of bacon pulled me from a sound sleep. My tail thumped against the floorboards, a rhythmic beat accompanying my eager trot to the kitchen. My human was already awake, their movements quiet and purposeful, the gentle clinking of pans a soothing melody. They looked down, a smile crinkling the corners of their eyes, and I received my reward: a small piece of crispy, delicious bacon. Sharing a piece of breakfast became a ritual, a silent acknowledgment of our growing bond.

It was not about the food; it was about the connection, the shared moment of quiet understanding. I learned to anticipate their movements, recognizing the subtle signs that heralded the beginning of our daily routine. The rustling of the pantry door, the creak of the cabinet, and the hum of the refrigerator became my cues, each promising delicious smells and joyful moments.

Our playtime was an explosion of energy. I had bounded across the living room, a whirlwind of fur and playful nips, while my human would laugh, their movements fluid and joyous as they engaged in my wild game of chase. I learned to respond to their laughter, interpreting its joyous sound as a sign of approval, a green light to continue my exuberant play. We wrestled on the rug in a joyful tangle of limbs and playful yelps. They tugged my ears, and I yelped in mock protest, a game we both loved. Those moments brimmed with pure joy, deepening our bond with every laugh.

Learning to sit and stay was not always easy. As I grew, my attention was quickly diverted by a butterfly or the scent of an earthworm. Frustration flickered in my human's eyes during these moments, but their patience remained steadfast. They did not raise their voice or use harsh methods; instead, they gently guided me with corrections and positive reinforcement. A treat for a successful "sit" and a word of praise for a moment of sustained attention. Each small victory felt momentous, a testament to our mutual effort and the blossoming understanding between us.

Slowly, I began to understand their language. "Sit," "Stay," "Come" –these words became anchors in my world, guiding my actions and earning me praise and affection. But beyond the formal commands, I started to understand the nuances of their communication. A soft tone meant gentleness, a playful one signaled a game, and a firm tone indicated a need for obedience. I learned to read their body language – the subtle shifts in their posture, the expressions in their eyes, and the way their hands moved. This silent language was as important as the spoken words, enriching our understanding and connection.

My human also began to understand me. The frantic wag of my tail signaled excitement; a soft whimper conveyed apprehension, and a deep bark announced a territorial warning. They learned to interpret the subtle shifts in my demeanor and the subtle nuances of my body language. They learned to recognize when I needed a cuddle, whether I was tired, excited, or ready for a game of fetch.

One evening, I curled up at their feet, watching them read. The warm glow of the lamplight illuminated their face, highlighting the lines of concentration etched on their brow. I rested my head on their legs, feeling the gentle rise and fall of their chest, the steady beat of their heart mirroring my own. It was not a dramatic moment, with no grand gestures or pronouncements; instead, it was a quiet sharing of peace and comfort. In these quiet moments, amidst the chaos of puppyhood and the rigors of training, our bond truly flourished.

Our walks became our shared adventures. The world outside our house unfolded before me in a riot of sensations, each a new experience to explore and understand. I learned to navigate the world alongside my human, my senses heightened, my focus sharp. The scents of the city—exhaust fumes, freshly baked bread, damp earth after a rain—created a rich olfactory tapestry, a complex puzzle I delighted in solving. The sounds of traffic, birdsong, and distant sirens—a symphony of urban life that I slowly began to decipher.

My human pointed out squirrels darting across the park, birds soaring high above, and butterflies fluttering amongst the flowers. They shared their observations of the world, explaining the names of the trees and plants and describing the behaviors of the animals. I would follow their gaze, absorbing their insights and connecting them to my sensory experiences. These moments became shared lessons, a collaborative exploration of our surroundings.

Our connection deepened through the challenges we faced together.

A minor illness, a sudden thunderstorm, or a moment of fear in the face of a large truck—each hurdle brought us closer, solidifying the trust that underpins our relationship. Their calm reassurances and gentle care taught me I was safe, protected, and loved. They were not my teacher and playmate; they were my rock and source of comfort and stability.

My human's patience and understanding extended beyond the playful moments. They recognized that my knowledge of their words and instructions gradually evolved. They celebrated every milestone, big or small, which reinforced my confidence and encouraged me to make further progress. Their teaching style was gentle yet firm, patient, and consistently positive, ensuring a harmonious learning experience. They did not expect perfection; they expected progress.

As the weeks turned into months, the clumsy puppy I once was transformed into a confident, intelligent young dog. I learned simple commands to interpret their emotions, subtle cues, and unspoken needs. My responses became more nuanced and refined: a soft nuzzle to offer comfort, a playful bark to initiate a game, and a quiet presence to provide companionship. It was a relationship built on mutual understanding and affection.

They were my guide, my protector, and my best friend. In my way, I strived to be worthy of their love and faith in me. As a puppy, full of boundless energy and insatiable curiosity, I knew this: I had found my human, and my life, filled with adventure, loyalty, and unwavering love, had only begun.

CHAPTER 3
The World Through Puppy Eyes

The moment I stepped through the back door, the world exploded into a symphony of scents. It was a far cry from the controlled environment of the house, a place of familiar smells: the comforting scent of my human's skin, the leathery aroma of their worn boots, and the faintly sweet smell of laundry detergent clinging to their clothes. Outside, however, the air thrummed with a vibrant, almost overwhelming cacophony of aromas.

First, the Earth. Rich, dark, and deeply satisfying, it filled my nostrils with a complex perfume of damp soil and decaying leaves. I sniffed deeply, my tail thumping a joyful rhythm against my rear legs. It was a scent of life, growth, and hidden mysteries buried beneath the surface. I dug my paws into the soft earth, relishing the cool, damp feeling between my toes. The texture was a revelation –unlike the smooth hardwood floors of the house, the earth yielded and shifted beneath my paws, offering a unique tactile experience.

Then came the grass. Tall, swaying blades tickled my nose and brushed against my fur, a delightful and oddly unfamiliar sensation. It smelled green, fresh, and alive, infused with the subtle scent of sunshine and dew. I rolled in it, delighting in the incredible softness as the blades brushed against my skin. The sensation was unlike anything I had experienced before, a thrilling explosion of touch. The grass offered a shifting landscape of textures, soft in some places, coarse in others, keeping my paws endlessly intrigued.

The air buzzed with a myriad of smells. Sweet honeysuckle perfume wafted from a nearby bush, its intoxicating fragrance pulling me closer. I sniffed delicately, letting the scent wash over me, a wave of floral delight. A more pungent aroma, earthy and musky, emanated from the base of an old oak tree. It smelled of hidden creatures, tiny lives teeming beneath the bark, a silent world unfolding beneath my nose.

Further afield, the scent of freshly cut grass hung in the air, sharp and invigorating. It was a clean, almost metallic scent, hinting at my human's work. The smell of distant woods, a blend of pine needles and damp earth, added another layer to this olfactory tapestry. It was a scent that promised adventure, beckoning me to explore further and delve deeper into the backyard's mysteries.

My ears were exposed to a continuous flow of sounds. Crickets chirping formed a constant background hum, a rhythmic pulse to the backyard's life. Birds sang their sweet melodies from the branches of trees, their cheerful chirps filling the air with joy. The buzzing of bees, a low, constant drone, added to the orchestra of nature. A distant lawnmower roared to life, its mechanical humming momentarily overpowering the natural sounds before fading into the background.

My eyes, still adjusting to the bright sunlight, took in the kaleidoscope of colors and shapes. The vibrant green of the grass contrasted sharply with the deep brown of the earth. The multi-hued leaves of the plants offered a riot of textures and shades. I watched a butterfly, its wings a kaleidoscope of colors, flitting from flower to flower. Its delicate movements were hypnotic and fascinating. I watched, mesmerized, as it danced amongst the blossoms, a speck of beauty against the backdrop of green.

The sun's movement on the leaves created an endless dance of light and shadow, transforming the backyard into a constantly shifting landscape. I discovered a warm and inviting patch of sunlight and lay down to bask in its glow. The feel of the sun's warmth on my fur was pure bliss. Exploring the backyard was an immersive sensory experience, a constant stream of information processed through my nose, ears, and eyes. It was a far more complex and prosperous world than I had encountered indoors. Every rustle of leaves, every bird chirp, every scent carried on the breeze – it was all part of this intricate tapestry of experience. I spent hours exploring, my senses heightened, my curiosity boundless. I chased butterflies, sniffed at flowers, dug in the earth, and explored every nook and cranny of the expansive outdoor realm before me. Each moment is a discovery. Each scent is a new adventure. Each sound is a revelation.

I discovered a small stream running at the yard's edge, its water gurgling gently. The cool, clean scent of the water was refreshing as I lapped at it with delight. Smooth, cool pebbles shifted under my paws, each step a tactile adventure. I chased a fat bumblebee from flower to flower, my body buzzing with the thrill of the chase. A squirrel darted up a tree, a blur of brown against the green. Through a puppy's eyes, the world was a heady wonderland of sights, sounds, and textures.

Of course, there were challenges. The occasional thorny bush would cause a yelp of surprise. The relentless buzzing of a particularly aggressive bee sent me scampering away, my tail between my legs. However, even these minor setbacks added to the thrill of exploration, serving as a reminder that this vast and exciting world held both pleasures and challenges. They were all part of the learning experience.

As dusk settled, painting the sky in hues of orange and purple, I felt a sense of accomplishment. I had explored, I had discovered, I had experienced. My backyard was no longer a space; it was my world, full of wonders to explore, sensory treasures to uncover, and adventures yet to come. And it was a world I was eager to share with my human. The day's adventures had brought us closer; our bond was strengthened by shared experiences and the thrill of discovery. Curled up at my human's feet, tired but content, I knew our adventures were only beginning. The scent of the earth, the chirping of crickets, the sun's warmth on my fur all would be woven into the tapestry of our shared memories, a lasting reminder of the boundless joy and wonder of my first days seeing the world through a puppy's eyes.

CHAPTER 4

First Steps in Obedience

The scent of kibble, usually a siren song, held little appeal that morning. My attention was riveted on a particularly intriguing butterfly, its wings a blur of iridescent colors against the vibrant green backdrop of the lawn. My human, however, had other plans. A small, brightly colored object appeared in their hand – a squeaky toy shaped like a bone. This, I quickly learned, was the prelude to something called "training."

The word itself held no meaning, but the tone in my human's voice —a mixture of patience and firmness —suggested a change in our routine. The bone-shaped toy was waved enticingly, followed by the word "Sit." My tail wagged furiously; I was accustomed to games, but this one felt different. My instinct was to pounce, snatch the toy, and engage in a joyful wrestling match. Instead, my human's hand remained steady, their voice calm but unwavering.

The frustration bubbled within me. The bone! So close! Yet, the tantalizing treat remained out of reach. I let out a low, rumbling whine, my chest vibrating with displeasure at this puzzling game. My attempts to distract myself—a quick sniff at a particularly enticing blade of grass, a furtive glance at a passing bird – were met with a gentle but firm redirection. "Sit," the word repeated, a gentle but insistent pressure on my rump guiding me into the desired position.

The first successful "Sit" was a victory for both of us. The bone-shaped toy was offered as a reward, a squeaky confirmation of my accomplishment. The taste of success was intoxicating. The tiny squeaks of the toy, combined with the taste of the reward, were immensely satisfying, and soon I started to connect the sound "sit" with the satisfying action of receiving the treat. My body, even amidst my initial confusion, was wired to learn. A single session was sufficient to grasp the fundamental principle of cause and effect. Sit = treat.

"Stay" proved to be more challenging. The lure of the backyard, its wealth of scents and sounds, was too tempting to resist. The word was barely uttered before I was bounding toward a particularly enticing patch of newly turned earth. The immediate correction, a gentle but firm "No," was met with a confused whimper. This was not a game I understood, a rule I did not instinctively follow. It took countless repetitions, distractions, and corrections, but gradually, the word "Stay" began to hold meaning.

Each successful "Stay," even if only for a few seconds, was celebrated with lavish praise and another squeaky bone. The longer I could resist the allure of the world outside, the more enthusiastic my human became, their praise escalating from a simple "Good boy" to enthusiastic clapping and petting. The positive reinforcement worked wonders; the reward was far better than any scent the backyard had to offer. It was a connection of love and understanding.

"Come" presented a different sort of challenge. My enthusiasm for this command was boundless; I loved the game of chase. However, it took time to learn that "Come" did not simply mean "run toward the sound of your name," but to come when called, regardless of how alluring a butterfly or squirrel might be. Several close calls with speeding cars and errant bicycles taught me the importance of unwavering obedience.

The lessons were not confined to the backyard. Walks became a series of mini-training sessions, each encounter with a new distraction—a stray dog, a passing bicycle, the enticing scent of a nearby bakery—an opportunity to reinforce "Sit," "Stay," and "Come." It was not always easy. Moments of frustration, where my puppy instincts overrode my training, were frequent. But my human's patience, their unwavering belief in my ability to learn, never wavered.

Over time, the commands became second nature. The frustration that marked the early days slowly gave way to accomplishment, a quiet pride in my ability to please my human. I began to anticipate their commands and understand the subtle cues in their posture and their voice. The training was not about learning words, but about building a connection —a language of mutual understanding that transcended mere obedience.

Our bond deepened with every successful command and every shared moment of triumph. I was not simply learning basic obedience; I was learning to communicate, cooperate, and work together as a team. The reward was not a squeaky bone; it was the unwavering affection in my human's eyes, the enthusiastic praise, the comforting touch of their hand.

Evenings were spent practicing "Down," a command that initially seemed impossible. My natural inclination was to stand tall and proud, my legs a pillar of youthful energy. The first few attempts ended in giggles from my human and much tumbling on my part.

Yet, my determination was matched by their patience. Each successful "Down" was met with a fervent outpouring of affection and a particularly juicy meat treat. One evening, amidst a flurry of "Downs" and "Sits," a new command was introduced: "Leave it." This was a test of wills, a battle against my powerful olfactory instincts. A juicy piece of chicken lay just out of reach, its aroma calling to me like a siren. My human's voice was firm, their hand steady as they held the morsel away. Desire for the treat warred with my need to obey. The struggle was long, but the victory was sweet when I finally obeyed. It was another step in our training, another stride toward our shared goal.

The transition from unruly puppy to attentive student was a gradual process, marked by both triumphs and setbacks. There were days when my attention span seemed nonexistent, when the allure of a butterfly or a passing squirrel proved too strong. There were days when frustration boiled over, and I responded with a playful nip or a stubborn refusal to obey. But through it all, my human's unwavering patience and positive reinforcement remained constant.

The training was not about teaching me commands but building a foundation of trust and understanding. It was about establishing a clear hierarchy, where my human was the leader, and I was the devoted follower. It was a journey of mutual learning, a dance between obedience and affection. Each successful command reinforced our bond, and each shared moment of laughter and success deepened our connection. By the time the first month of our training journey concluded, we had made remarkable progress, establishing a strong foundation for the future challenges we were set to overcome. The scent of adventures ahead—adventures that stretched far beyond the backyard—was almost as compelling as the smell of the delicious treats. My training was ultimately rewarding. The path to becoming a search and rescue dog was long, yet the journey, step by step, was one filled with mutual love and exhilarating adventures.

CHAPTER 5
The Joy of Play and Companionship

The sun, a warm hand on my fur, woke me. The scent of bacon, sharp and delicious, drifted from the kitchen, a powerful motivator even before my eyes were fully open. My human, their hair still tousled from sleep, greeted me with a cheerful "Good morning!" and a scratch behind the ears, a ritual that instantly transformed my tail into a blur of happy motion. Breakfast was a flurry of enthusiastic gulps, a reward for a good night's sleep, punctuated by happy sighs and contented licks.

After breakfast, the routine began. The training wasn't a chore; it was an adventure, a game of wits and obedience, where the reward was not a tasty treat but a warm approval in my human's eyes. We started with the basics: "Sit," "Stay," and "Come," each commanding a challenge, each successful execution, and a victory celebrated with enthusiastic praise and a satisfying chew toy. I learned to anticipate their commands, the subtle shifts in their body language a silent prelude to the next instruction. It was not about blind obedience; it was a dance, a partnership forged in mutual understanding and shared joy.

My human's patience was endless, their corrections gentle yet firm. There were moments of frustration, of course. My puppyish exuberance sometimes got the better of me, leading to playful nips and enthusiastic attempts to chase squirrels that often ended in a gentle reprimand and a return to our exercises. But even these moments were woven into the tapestry of our growing bond. They were lessons in self-control, understanding boundaries, and focusing on the task.

The backyard, my playground, became our training ground. The world was a symphony of intriguing scents and sounds: the rustle of leaves, the chirping of birds, and the busy hum of the neighbor's lawnmower. Each distraction was a test, a challenge to my developing focus, and a lesson in self-control.

My human's guidance transformed these distractions into opportunities to strengthen my obedience, each successful "Stay" amidst a flurry of tempting distractions a testament to our growing teamwork.

Mid-morning brought a welcome break from training. The family gathered for a leisurely game of fetch in the park, a joyful ballet of flying frisbees and enthusiastic leaps. The pure, unadulterated joy of the game filled me with a heady rush of excitement. The simple pleasures that filled my days with boundless happiness were the feel of the grass beneath my paws, the exhilaration of the chase, and the thrill of catching the Frisbee.

The afternoon consisted of more training, but it was infused with a playful energy that made the learning experience exciting. My human incorporated new commands, like "Down" and "Leave it," each a step further along the path of becoming a proficient working dog. "Leave it" was particularly challenging, requiring self-control that demanded immense patience and persistence. The aroma of a particularly delicious piece of roast chicken wafting from the kitchen was a formidable opponent, but the reward of mastering the command far outweighed any immediate temptation.

Evenings were spent with family. The warm glow of the living room, the soft sounds of conversation, and the comforting presence of my human filled my heart with love. I would curl up at their feet, a furry warmth against their skin, basking in their affection, with the rhythmic sound of their heartbeat as a soothing lullaby.

Weekends brought extended adventures. Hikes in the woods, where the scents were intoxicating, the terrain challenging, and the sheer joy of exploration endless. These were times when my training truly came alive. My human, ever vigilant, would call out commands –"Come," "Stay," "Leave it" – each command seamlessly integrated into our shared experience. It was a testament to the foundation of trust and understanding we had built.

The bond between us deepened not through training but through shared experiences. The laughter during playtime, the quiet companionship of evening cuddles, and shared adventures in the woods all contributed to building our relationship, transforming a simple owner-dog bond into a deep, lasting friendship. I was learning obedience, love, trust, and teamwork.

The more I learned, the more my human praised me, and the greater my desire to please them became. Each successful command reaffirmed our bond, a mutual achievement celebrated with joyful exuberance. The reward system my human employed was not simply about treats; it was about the genuine affection in their eyes, the heartfelt praise, and the warm touch of their hands. My successes were theirs just as much as they were mine.

One memorable afternoon, a small child dropped their ice cream while we played in the park. Their sudden cries cut through the air, and soon their distressed parents joined the search. Before I even realized it, I was sniffing the ground, following the faint scent of melting strawberries. I paused, focused, then bolted in a determined dash. Moments later, I found the fallen treat and nudged it gently with my nose, proudly returning it to the family with my tail wagging furiously. The parents were visibly relieved, their gratitude radiating warmth deep into my soul. It was a simple act, but it was a preview of things to come – a tiny glimpse into the role I would one day play in helping those in need.

As the weeks turned into months, my training intensified. New commands were introduced, more complex exercises were mastered, and each hurdle was overcome, bringing me a step closer to my goal. The focus shifted from basic obedience to more specialized tasks, preparing me for the challenges ahead – challenges that I was eager to face, driven not by duty but by an overwhelming desire to serve.

The joy of learning and pleasing my human, intertwined with the satisfaction of successful training, painted my days in a spectrum of fulfillment I had only begun to comprehend. The love and laughter within our family were as essential a part of my development as the rigorous training itself. The balance between work and play, obedience, and affection was the perfect recipe for shaping me into the dog I was destined to be – a rescue dog, ready to embrace whatever adventure awaited.

CHAPTER 6

Growing Up and Getting Serious

My first birthday arrived like a whirlwind of excitement. One minute, I was a clumsy, playful pup; the next, I was a leaner, more powerful dog, my once-floppy ears now standing tall, my gait more confident, and my body more defined. The changes were not physical; my mental acuity had sharpened, my understanding of commands refined, and my ability to focus intensified. My human's playful tone during training had not disappeared; it was interwoven with a new sense of purpose, a gravity that matched my maturity.

The backyard training sessions became increasingly demanding. The simple commands "sit" and "stay" were replaced with more complex exercises that involved longer durations, heightened distractions, and more precise execution. The agility courses my human introduced formed a maze of jumps and tunnels that tested my coordination, speed, and ability to follow instructions under pressure. The scent work intensified, requiring me to distinguish between subtly different aromas and trace them with precision and focus. My human introduced me to the concept of "area search," a fundamental skill in search and rescue, teaching me to systematically cover ground while using my nose to detect the faintest trace of a scent.

The training was not about physical skill but mental fortitude. My human pushed me beyond my comfort zone, challenging my stamina, patience, and determination. There were moments of frustration when I struggled and faltered, and the sheer complexity of the tasks seemed overwhelming. But these moments were crucial. They were not failures but growth opportunities for learning, pushing my limits, and discovering the depths of my resilience. My human's support, encouragement, and corrections helped me overcome challenges and become more confident. They celebrated my successes as much as they guided me through my setbacks, teaching me that perseverance, not perfection, was the key to mastery. One particularly challenging exercise involved searching for a hidden object in a large, wooded area. The scent was faint, obscured by the numerous other scents in the forest, and the terrain was uneven and challenging. I struggled, distracted by the abundance of smells – a rabbit, a deer, a decaying log – each vying for my attention. My human remained patient, their encouragement constant, reminding me to focus, cover the area, and trust my nose systematically.

Finally, after what felt like an eternity, I caught a whiff of the object – a worn leather glove – and bounded towards it, tail wagging, barking excitedly. My human's smile was radiant, their praise echoing through the woods. That day, I learned something profoundly important: even when the task seems impossible, persistent effort and unwavering self-belief can lead to remarkable success.

My human's choice to pursue search and rescue training was deliberate. It wasn't about simple obedience or basic agility; it was about directing my abilities toward something meaningful and life-affirming. It was about using my unique talents to help others, save lives, and be part of something larger than myself. The decision also signified a shift in our relationship. Our bond was not about shared play and comforting companionship; it was now about a shared purpose and commitment to something beyond the ordinary.

The increased intensity of my training was not merely a matter of longer sessions or more challenging tasks but a reflection of the gravity of the mission ahead. It felt different now; there was a deeper purpose, an underlying current of responsibility. The playful exuberance we shared remained, but now it was tempered by a growing awareness of the seriousness of my training, of the weight of what was to come. My human's commitment to this training was as strong as my own, and as the weeks passed into months, I realized that this wasn't merely about becoming a well-trained dog. It was about becoming a partner, a teammate, a lifesaver.

My human introduced me to other search and rescue dogs and their handlers. These dogs were incredible, focused, disciplined, and incredibly skilled craft masters. Watching them work and their unwavering dedication instilled in me awe and a profound desire to emulate their example. The camaraderie among the handlers was heartwarming as well – a shared understanding, mutual respect, and a deep appreciation for the unique capabilities of their canine companions. This environment further solidified my resolve to pursue this path; I was not merely becoming a search and rescue dog but joining a dedicated and supportive community.

The transition from a playful puppy to a serious, working dog was gradual, marked by a growing sense of responsibility. The joyful moments of fetch in the park and the cozy evenings curled by the fire remained vital to our relationship, a balance to the intense rigors of my training. These moments of affection and play were not breaks; they were essential components, recharging my spirit, reminding me of the core of our bond, and sustaining my motivation. They also served as opportunities for my human to reinforce our connection on a personal level, ensuring that amidst the focus and intensity of our training, the essence of our companionship remained unshaken.

As my first birthday approached, training became more frequent and intense. My body grew stronger, my stamina improved, and obedience became almost instinctive. I learned to read my human's subtle cues, anticipating commands before they were spoken, displaying a level of coordination and teamwork I hadn't known I possessed. The scent work became increasingly complex; I learned to differentiate between the subtle nuances of various scents, tracing them through the most challenging environments and navigating obstacles and distractions with growing confidence.

One of the most crucial aspects of my training was the development of my emotional intelligence, which required a different approach than physical agility or scent work. My human emphasized impulse control, teaching me to remain calm under stress and to follow instructions even when faced with distracting situations. This part of the training was particularly important, as the search and rescue work often involves high-pressure, emotionally charged scenarios. Managing my reactions, maintaining my focus, and performing effectively under pressure was more important than being the fastest or most agile.

The decision to pursue search and rescue was not solely my human's; it was a shared understanding, a mutual agreement forged in our bond. It was not about fulfilling a role but about embracing destiny. My human's trust in me and my desire to serve and to please them became interwoven, propelling me to push beyond my physical and mental limits. Our understanding transcended a simple training routine; it was a powerful partnership built on trust, respect, and a deep, abiding love.

My training was not a solitary endeavor but a shared adventure, a dance of mutual understanding and reciprocal growth. My dedication and patience were mirrored by my unwavering commitment to mastering each new skill and challenge. The countless hours spent honing my abilities, the steadfast support, the shared moments of frustration, and the ultimate triumph all cemented the foundation of our partnership. We were more than a dog and a human; we were a team, forging an unbreakable bond rooted in mutual respect and shared purpose. Our training was not about preparing me for the work ahead; it was about solidifying the connection between us, proving that we could face whatever lay ahead through mutual devotion and unwavering perseverance.

The journey from a carefree puppy to a dedicated search and rescue dog was a transformative one. It was not simply about mastering commands and perfecting skills; it was about the evolution of a bond, the emergence of a partnership, and the discovery of a shared purpose far more significant than we could have imagined. The chapters will detail the thrilling missions, the emotional highs and lows, and the rewards and challenges of this incredible journey. However, this foundational chapter highlights the crucial groundwork, meticulous training, and the profound bond that formed the basis for everything that came after. It was a journey built on patience, trust, and an unshakeable love that would fuel our journey together, shaping us into the dynamic duo we were destined to be.

CHAPTER 7
Meeting the Team

The crisp autumn air nipped at my nose as we arrived at the training grounds. It was not my human and me anymore; we were part of something larger, something far more exhilarating. The air hummed with vibrant energy, a symphony of barking, excited yips, and the comforting murmur of human voices. Before me lay a sprawling field, a vibrant tapestry of activity. Dogs of all shapes and sizes, each with a unique blend of muscle and grace, were engaged in various exercises, their movements precise and powerful. Golden Retrievers, sleek and elegant, effortlessly navigated intricate obstacle courses. Labradors, with their boundless energy, bounded through tunnels with joyous abandon. Border Collies, masters of agility, zipped through jumps with incredible speed and precision.

And then there were the other German Shepherds, their proud bearing reflecting their inherent strength and intelligence. They moved with an almost supernatural grace, each stride purposeful, each movement economical. My human introduced me to the team, a diverse and captivating group. Ranger, a majestic black Labrador with unwavering focus, and his handler, a seasoned veteran named Sarah, exuded a quiet confidence that mirrored her canine partner's calm demeanor. Ranger possessed an almost uncanny ability to locate scents deep within the most challenging terrains. He earned a reputation for finding people lost in the wilderness, seemingly sniffing out hope itself. His presence radiated calm assurance, a quality that seemed to permeate those around him. Sarah, in turn, embodied unwavering support, her gentle words and encouraging touch perfectly complementing Ranger's steadfast nature. Their connection was not merely that of a handler and her dog; it was a partnership built on mutual respect and years of shared success, a powerful testament to dedication and loyalty.

Then there was Luna, a spirited Border Collie with boundless energy and a mischievous glint in her bright eyes. Her handler, Mark, a young man, possessed an infectious enthusiasm that mirrored Luna's vibrant spirit. Luna was a whirlwind of activity, a blur of controlled motion, as she conquered the agility courses with the kind of speed that stole your breath and grace that seemed effortless. Watching her was like witnessing a finely tuned machine perfectly balanced between power and grace. Mark's handling was equally impressive; his movements were fluid and intuitive, with a seamless interplay between the human and canine partners. He seemed to anticipate Luna's every move, guiding her with effortless precision, a beautiful synergy of partnership. Their bond crackled with energy; it was palpable and infectious, illustrating their years of close collaboration and mutual trust.

Further down the field, I met a pair that defied my expectations. This was Rocky, a sturdy, scruffy-looking mixed breed, his coat a patchwork of browns and tans, far from the picture-perfect image of a search-and-rescue dog. But something was compelling about him; his eyes held an intelligence that belied his unkempt appearance. His handler, a quiet woman named Emily, seemed to understand him completely, communicating through subtle gestures and soft tones that only she and Rocky appeared to comprehend. Rocky was, without a doubt, the most unexpected member of the team. His unorthodox appearance stood in stark contrast to his exceptional abilities. He lacked the sleekness of a Labrador or the agility of a Border Collie, but he had relentless determination and an uncanny ability to track scent. His and Emily's partnership was a testament to that in search and rescue, what truly mattered was not the outward appearance but an unwavering bond and unwavering dedication.

The air crackled with a palpable sense of camaraderie. The handlers were not individuals; they were a team, a cohesive unit bound by a shared purpose and a deep respect for each other's canine partners. Their interactions were marked by mutual respect, a quiet understanding, an unspoken language of shared experience, and challenges overcome. They shared stories, offered advice, celebrated successes, and provided comfort during moments of disappointment. This was more than a training ground; it was a community, a family forged in the crucible of challenging training and shared purpose.

As I observed these dogs and their handlers, I realized that search and rescue was not merely a job; it was a vocation, a calling that demanded dedication, skill, and an unbreakable bond between humans and animals. I observed how the handlers interacted with their dogs, noting their tone of voice, gestures, and how they acknowledged the dogs' achievements – all of which spoke to a profound connection beyond simple obedience. It was evident that they had an exceptional level of empathy and an ability to understand the needs and emotions of their canine partners. Their sensitivity and understanding reinforced a powerful bond, creating a foundation of trust critical for success in this challenging and often emotionally demanding work.

Each dog, in its unique way, reflected the character of its human companion. Ranger's calm steadiness reflected Sarah's composure, Luna's boundless energy echoed Mark's enthusiasm, and Rocky's quiet determination mirrored Emily's patient understanding. There was an undeniable harmony between each canine partner and their human, reflecting years of training, mutual trust, and a shared commitment to a higher purpose.

That day, I learned more than new commands or techniques. I learned about teamwork, community, and the incredible bond between humans and their canine partners. I witnessed the depth of dedication, unwavering commitment, and quiet strength of these extraordinary individuals and their animals. They were a testament to the power of shared purpose and the incredible achievements that could be realized through mutual trust and unwavering loyalty.

The training continued throughout the day. We practiced various search techniques, with each dog demonstrating its unique strengths. Ranger's methodical approach was a testament to his experience, and his unwavering focus was a marvel to behold. Luna's speed and agility were breathtaking, and her effortless navigation of the obstacle courses was a testament to her exceptional skills. Despite his unorthodox appearance, Rocky consistently proved his capability, and his determination and unwavering focus made him an unlikely yet valuable asset to the team. I learned from them, observing their techniques, strategies, and ability to overcome obstacles and persist despite the challenges.

The other dogs and I quickly bonded, forming a silent understanding through our shared, intense training experience. A playful rivalry emerged—a friendly competition fueled by our mutual desire to outdo each other. However, it was also rooted in respect and camaraderie; we were all together. We recognized the inherent value of teamwork, the significance of relying on one another, and the collective strength that resulted from our combined abilities.

As the sun began to dip below the horizon, casting long shadows across the training field, I felt a sense of contentment. I was not a dog undergoing training; I was part of something larger: a remarkable team member. This was not merely a job; it was a vocation, a calling that blended the thrill of adventure, the satisfaction of accomplishment, and the immeasurable reward of knowing that I could use my abilities to make a real difference in the world. It was all underpinned by the extraordinary bond I shared with my human, which fueled my dedication, inspired my perseverance, and made this challenging yet enriching journey possible. This was the beginning of my life's work, a chapter that promised excitement, challenges, and the profound satisfaction of serving alongside these exceptional individuals and their equally remarkable canine partners. The journey had begun, and I was ready.

CHAPTER 8
Agility Training Begins

The following day dawned crisp and clear, the sun painting the dew-kissed grass in shades of gold and amber. Agility training commenced, marking the start of a new phase in my life. It wasn't about running and jumping anymore; it was about precision, control, and the unwavering trust between my human and me. The agility course loomed before me, a daunting array of obstacles designed to evaluate the limits of both our physical and mental capabilities. A low tunnel, barely high enough for me to crawl through, beckoned first. My human, calm, and reassuring voice guided me through, his hand putting gentle pressure on my back as I navigated the tight confines.

The scent of freshly turned earth filled my nostrils as I emerged, the cool dampness clinging to my fur. Next was a series of jumps, varying in height, which evaluated my coordination and judgment. At first, I hesitated, my instincts telling me to leap over the hurdles in a flurry of uncontrolled energy. But my human's patient guidance, his quiet commands punctuated by gentle encouragement, taught me to approach each jump with calculated precision, each landing a testament to my growing skill. I learned to pace myself, use my momentum wisely, and judge distances perfectly. Each successful jump was a small victory, a boost to my confidence, strengthening the bond between my human and me.

Then came the teeter-totter, a wobbly wooden plank poised precariously over a small gap. My instincts screamed caution, but my human's calm voice instilled trust. He lured me forward with a small piece of kibble, his touch light and encouraging. It was nerve-wracking, but I gradually gained confidence, and we perfected the balancing act, our movements becoming increasingly synchronized. The teeter-totter became a testament to our growing teamwork.

The A-frame, a steep incline leading to a narrow peak, presented a new challenge. My human demonstrated the route, his gait steady and confident. I watched him absorb his approach and the subtle shifts in his body that enabled him to maintain balance. Following his instructions, I climbed, my claws gripping the rough surface. The higher I climbed, the more exhilarating it became.

Reaching the top and surveying the course from my lofty perch filled me with accomplishment. The descent, though steep, was a smooth exercise of controlled movement, my human's support guiding my every step. The tire jump was the most daunting obstacle. The large tire, its rubber surface strangely smooth, seemed to mock my abilities. I sniffed it cautiously, my nose twitching as I assessed its size. My human patiently showed me how to approach, position myself, and gather my momentum before launching. With each attempt, I improved, my jumps becoming more powerful and my landings smoother. By the end of the session, I was navigating the tire with an almost effortless grace, my leaps becoming increasingly fluid and powerful.

The slender and close-set weave poles required more than speed; they demanded agility, precision, and a keen understanding of spatial awareness. My human patiently guided me, his voice a constant hum of encouragement, his movements subtle and guiding. At first, my progress was clumsy, my movements halting and hesitant. But gradually, with his positive feedback, my pace improved, the weave poles morphing into a rhythmic dance between my human and me.

Days turned into weeks, weeks into months. My training progressed, and my skills sharpened. I remember the frustration of failing and the moments of doubt and insecurity. But my human's unwavering support, patience, and understanding never faltered. He celebrated my successes and gently encouraged me through my mistakes. There was no harshness, only kindness and unwavering belief in my abilities. He adjusted the training to my learning pace, ensuring the sessions were both challenging and enjoyable.

My keen sense of smell was honed through scent discrimination exercises. I learned to distinguish between different scents, follow specific trails, and identify particular objects. My human hid treats and toys, testing my ability to find them and gradually increasing the challenge. The harder the task, the more focused and determined I became, reflecting the strong partnership we had built. The physical training was equally demanding. We ran through fields, hills, and forests, building my stamina and strengthening my muscles. My body became leaner and more powerful, capable of sustained effort and rapid bursts of speed. We trained in rain, sun, snow, and heat.

The rigorous training was tough, but my human-assured intensity was always matched by care and attention to my fitness levels and well-being. Agility training was more than a series of physical challenges; it was a crucial step in my development as a search and rescue dog. It taught me obedience, precision, stamina, and unwavering focus. It was a testament to our bond, as well as our ability to work together as a cohesive unit, and our mutual understanding and respect. More than that, it constantly reinforced my trust in my human and his trust in me. We were a team, a partnership forged in the fires of intense training, a bond that would carry us through the demanding challenges ahead. The call of duty was coming, and we were ready.

CHAPTER 9
Mastering Obedience for the Field

The scent of pine and damp earth filled my nostrils as my human and I entered the training grounds. This was not the playful agility course but the crucible where obedience would be forged into an unbreakable bond. Here, amidst the controlled chaos of distractions, our teamwork would be tested to its limits. The initial exercises were familiar—sit, stay, come—but the stakes were higher. My human's commands were crisp, clear, and imbued with an urgency I'd not encountered before. He did not want me to sit; he needed me to sit instantly, reliably, even when a squadron of squirrels performed acrobatic feats beyond my reach.

Initially, the squirrels, the rustling leaves, and the distant barking of other dogs – all were powerful distractions. My youthful enthusiasm often led me astray. A tempting scent would distract my attention from my human commands, resulting in a gentle but firm correction. My human never raised his voice; his disappointment was a more powerful motivator than any shout. He understood my nature – a playful, inquisitive puppy – and adjusted the training, gradually increasing the difficulty of the distractions.

We progressed from simple commands in quiet settings to complex exercises in increasingly challenging environments. He introduced loud noises – the bang of a starter pistol, the blare of a car horn, the sharp crackle of a radio – all designed to test my ability to remain focused on his instructions. I remember one particularly challenging session where he scattered my favorite treats across the training field while a loud construction vehicle rumbled nearby. The scent of those treats was a siren song, but my human's voice, unwavering and reassuring, cut through the noise. The struggle was real, the temptation overwhelming, but I slowly and patiently learned to prioritize his commands above all else.

Precise recall became paramount. This was not about coming when called; it was about coming immediately, no matter the distraction, even if it meant foregoing a particularly enticing scent or a tempting game of chase. He would send me off on a simulated search, my nose glued to the ground, following a faint scent trail. Then, he would call me back at a crucial moment – not a casual "come here," but a sharp, urgent command. The training became a dance between obedience and freedom, between the allure of the scent and the security of my human's presence. My reward was not praise but the comfort of his touch, the silent reassurance of his steady hand.

We progressed to heeling exercises, walking in perfect sync alongside him. He taught me to maintain a precise distance, responding instantaneously to his pace and direction changes. This was not merely about walking; it was about unwavering attention, about being constantly aware of his position, his movements, and his intentions. The training incorporated various obstacles—narrow pathways, uneven terrain, and sudden changes in elevation —designed to test my ability to maintain my position and focus.

The importance of 'stay' became painfully clear during a rigorous exercise. My human placed me in a 'stay' command amidst a flurry of activity—other dogs running, people shouting, and the ground vibrating with the sounds of passing vehicles. He then walked some distance away, eventually out of my sight, evaluating my willingness to remain precisely where he had left me despite the overwhelming sensory input. It was a test not merely of my obedience, but also my trust in Him, my faith in His return. Those moments of intense quiet while he was gone were a lesson in self-control, in the crucial importance of patience and discipline.

His eventual return was always met with unrestrained joy, a testament to the unwavering bond we were building. The training was not about responding to commands; it was about anticipating his needs, interpreting his subtle cues, and working as a team to move seamlessly in sync with each other. We practiced simulated search and rescue scenarios, where I had to locate a hidden "victim" – usually a person hidden in dense underbrush or behind obstacles. The key was not finding the victim but remaining under control, responding to my handler's commands, even under pressure.

One such scenario involved a mock disaster scene with staged wreckage and simulated casualties. The sounds were cacophonous; the smells were overwhelmingly complex, a cocktail of fear, injury, and decay. I had to find the injured person amidst this chaos and then, crucially, remain calm and under control, awaiting my human's instructions before approaching. My initial instinct was to rush in immediately, but his calm commands, delivered amidst the chaos, pulled me back. It was a powerful demonstration of the value of precise obedience, not as a skill but as a critical life-saving measure.

These scenarios highlighted the critical nature of obedience in a search and rescue context. A dog's enthusiasm, if uncontrolled, can be as dangerous as a lack of initiative. My human's training was not simply about achieving perfect obedience; it was about refining my innate abilities, tempering my instincts, and ensuring my actions were always safe, effective, and under precise control.

The culmination of this intense training was a final assessment, a rigorous evaluation of my skills. It evaluated my recall, healing, ability to navigate complex environments, and proficiency in scent detection – all under pressure. The judges, experienced search and rescue professionals, observed my every move, scrutinizing my reactions and assessing my ability to work as part of a team. I passed the assessment with flying colors. It was not merely a matter of passing a test but a testament to the countless hours of dedication, the unwavering partnership, and the mutual trust that had transformed a playful puppy into a highly skilled search and rescue dog.

The feeling of accomplishment was immense —a powerful surge of pride and happiness, a tangible expression of our shared journey. It was a testament not to my abilities but also my human patience, his dedication, and his unwavering belief in my potential. The call of duty was no longer a distant echo; it was a tangible reality, and we were ready. We stood poised, ready to answer that call, a team forged in the fires of dedicated training, prepared to face whatever challenges lay ahead. The bond between us, strengthened by the rigors of advanced obedience, was the bedrock of our success.

CHAPTER 10

Scent Work: A New Skill Set

My human's sharp and familiar scent was my constant companion during the early stages of scent work. However, the challenge was now different. It was not about recognizing his scent amidst a field of distractions; it was about isolating a completely unknown human scent-a stranger's trace—from the complex olfactory tapestry of the world around me. The training ground was transformed. The controlled exercises were gone, replaced by a series of increasingly complex scenarios designed to evaluate my nascent ability to detect and track human scent.

My first lesson involved a simple game of hide-and-seek. My human hid behind a large oak tree, leaving behind a small piece of his clothing – a cotton handkerchief. My nose, twitching with anticipation, scoured the ground, sniffing the earth, the leaves, and the bark of the trees. The scent, faint at first, whispered on the wind, a subtle anomaly in the air. I followed it, tail wagging, body low to the ground, senses locked on the trail. A rush of exhilaration washed over me when I found him. The reward, his enthusiastic praise and a hearty scratch behind the ears, fueled my growing passion.

The exercises gradually grew more challenging. Instead of a single hiding spot, my human started leaving scent trails. These were not straight lines; they were winding paths, weaving through bushes, across open fields, and sometimes circling back on themselves. The complexity of the trails increased, introducing multiple scents – animal droppings, decaying leaves, the faint perfume of wildflowers – all designed to evaluate my ability to filter out the irrelevant and focus on the human scent. I learned to discern subtleties, recognize the unique signature of a human's scent, and trace its invisible thread through a cacophony of other olfactory stimuli.

We moved from simple trails to simulated search scenarios. These involved searching for a hidden "victim" – a person hidden within a designated area – amidst increasingly complex environments. One scenario unfolded in a dense forest, the air thick with the scents of pine needles and damp earth. The scent of decaying leaves mingled with the faint, almost imperceptible trace of a human presence. My nose worked tirelessly, sifting through the layers of smells; my body moved with fluid grace, my focus unwavering. I navigated obstacles – fallen logs, tangled undergrowth, steep inclines –following the faintest trace, driven by the intrinsic reward of the search, the thrill of the hunt, and the desire to please my human.

The success of these scenarios was not about finding the hidden individual; it was about doing so efficiently and accurately. I learned to indicate my findings to my human with a clear signal – a gentle sit or a focused stare at the location – a precise action honed through repetition and reinforcement. My human's guidance was pivotal. His calm, clear instructions, positive reinforcement, patience in correcting my mistakes, and unwavering belief in my abilities were instrumental to my success. He understood my enthusiasm and tendency to rush headlong into a task. He taught me the importance of systematic, methodical searching, careful investigation, and patience in the face of a challenging scent trail.

As I progressed, the scenarios became increasingly realistic. We started incorporating distractions. Other dogs would be running nearby, their scents mixing with the one I was tracking, creating a confusing olfactory landscape. Loud noises – simulated emergency sirens, the clamor of a crowd – were added to evaluate my focus and resilience. The intensity of these training sessions mirrored the chaotic reality of a real-world search and rescue operation, preparing me not only for the physical demands but also for the mental fortitude required to operate effectively under pressure.

One particularly challenging exercise involved searching for a scent trail in a bustling city park. The air was thick with a mixture of fragrances: exhaust fumes, hot dogs, popcorn, flowers, and the lingering scent of a thousand different people. The scent I was tracking – a faint trace left on a discarded tissue – was practically buried in this aromatic stew. The concentration required was immense, the mental strain considerable, but my training had prepared me well. I moved through the crowds, navigating around people, bicycles, and strollers, my nose glued to the ground as I diligently followed the subtle, almost imperceptible trail. The reward for locating the hidden item was enormous. It was not the praise from my human, but the satisfaction of knowing that I had overcome a significant obstacle and mastered a crucial skill.

The training also focused on distinguishing the scents of living individuals from those of the deceased. This proved the most challenging, demanding extreme concentration and sensitivity. The scent of a deceased person is subtle, often masked by the odors of decomposition. The exercises required careful analysis of various scents, focusing on the slightest variations. It was a profound lesson in responsibility and empathy, underscoring the gravity of the work ahead.

The mastery of scent work was not a skill; it was a transformation. It was about harnessing my innate abilities, refining my senses, and channeling my instincts into a precisely honed tool. It was about developing a profound understanding of the olfactory world, the ability to decode its complexities, and the confidence to rely on my senses to navigate challenging and potentially life-threatening situations. The scent work training was not preparation for a future role but a fundamental component of my transformation into a fully-fledged search and rescue dog. My senses, once simply a source of playful exploration, were now instruments of precision and life-saving power. The call of duty, once a distant echo, was now a tangible reality, and I stood ready to answer, my nose to the ground, my senses alert, prepared to find those lost and in need. My bond with my human was a testament to our training and a powerful force, amplifying my capabilities and ensuring our ability to work as a seamless, life-saving team.

CHAPTER 11
Area Search Techniques

The next phase of my training focused on area searches. It was no longer about following a scent trail; it was about systematically covering a designated area, a vast and unknown landscape, and searching for a single, elusive scent. My human introduced me to different search patterns–the parallel search, the grid search, the spiral search – each designed to cover the ground efficiently and thoroughly. The parallel search was straightforward: I had run back and forth across the designated area, my nose close to the ground, systematically covering each strip. The grid search was more complex, involving a more intricate pattern of overlapping squares that ensured no space was left unsearched. The spiral search, on the other hand, was ideal for situations where the starting point of the scent was unknown, enabling me to radiate outwards from a central point.

Each pattern required a different approach and a different level of concentration. The parallel search was relatively simple, demanding consistent speed and focus. The grid search needed more precision and spatial awareness, necessitating that I maintain a consistent distance between my search lines. The spiral search, however, was the most challenging, requiring a constant adjustment of my search radius to maintain an outward expansion while keeping track of the area already covered. The training was relentless. Day after day, we practiced in different environments – grassy fields, dense forests, rocky terrains. Each environment presented its unique challenges.

The grassy fields were deceptively complex. The wind often shifted the scent, making it difficult to track. The tall grass obstructed my view, and other animals – squirrels, rabbits, birds – added to the olfactory confusion. I learned to filter out these extraneous scents, focusing on the subtle human scent I was trained to find. The dense forests were even more challenging. The undergrowth was thick, the terrain uneven, and the air thick with the smell of pine needles, damp earth, and decaying leaves. Navigation became as crucial as scent detection, requiring me to carefully negotiate fallen logs, tangled undergrowth, and steep inclines.

The rocky terrains were the most physically demanding. The rough ground made it difficult to maintain a consistent search pattern, and the rocks often obscured the scent trail. I learned to adapt my search technique, sometimes using my paws to move aside loose rocks, carefully sniffing around the base of larger rocks, and occasionally climbing over more minor obstacles. I have learned to conserve energy, pace myself, and recognize when a break is needed.

The training also involved progressively more complex scenarios. Initially, the searches were simple, with a single "victim" hidden in a relatively small area. Gradually, the areas expanded, the number of "victims" increased, and the scenarios became more realistic. We moved from simple hide-and-seek games to simulations involving multiple "victims" hidden in various parts of an extensive search area. We practiced in different weather conditions, including rain, wind, and snow, each presenting its unique challenges. The wind, for instance, could disperse or distort the scent trail, making tracking more difficult. Rain often washed away or diluted scents, making the search more challenging. Snow, conversely, would preserve the scent trail but also make it harder to navigate the terrain.

Through it all, my human remained my steadfast guide. His calm, reassuring presence, clear instructions, and unwavering belief in my abilities kept me focused and motivated. He explained the logic behind each search pattern, teaching me to read the terrain, account for wind direction, and interpret the subtle cues of the scent trails. His patience was endless. He never scolded me for mistakes but instead used them as opportunities for learning, gently correcting my errors and reinforcing the correct techniques.

The most challenging aspect of area searching was learning to prioritize. I could easily be overwhelmed by the sheer volume of scents in an extensive search area. My human taught me to filter out irrelevant scents and concentrate on the most promising leads. This involved developing a sophisticated understanding of the olfactory landscape, learning to distinguish between various scents, and prioritizing those most likely to lead to a successful outcome. This involved distinguishing between animal tracks, human scents, and the many other olfactory details a landscape could contain.

One training exercise stands out in my memory. It was a full-day exercise in a sprawling park. Several "victims" were hidden within a large, wooded area, each representing a different challenge – one was hidden under dense foliage, another near a busy path, and a third near a body of water. I had to systematically cover the entire area, switching between search patterns as needed and adapting my technique to the terrain. It was physically and mentally exhausting, requiring constant concentration, sharp decision-making, and the ability to handle pressure. However, the satisfaction of locating each "victim" was immense – a profound sense of accomplishment fueled by the knowledge that I was making progress toward my goal.

This training honed my skills beyond simple scent detection. It developed my spatial awareness, problem-solving skills, and ability to work independently. It taught me to make quick, informed decisions, to adapt to changing circumstances, and to persevere even when faced with setbacks. I learned to trust my instincts, rely on my senses, and utilize my innate abilities to their fullest potential. The area search training was more than just practice; it was a crucible that forged my abilities, shaping me into the skilled and dependable search and rescue dog I was meant to be.

The feeling of accomplishment, the satisfaction of a successful search, the knowledge that my skills could make a real difference in the lives of others—these are the things that drive me. This journey was not merely about mastering a technique but discovering my purpose. Once, a faint whisper, the scent of a missing person now called to me with powerful clarity, a siren song guiding me toward my life's work.

CHAPTER 12

Building Confidence and Trust

Beyond the rigorous physical training and the complex strategies of area searching lies the foundation of our success: the unbreakable bond between handler and dog. It was about me mastering techniques and forging a partnership built on unwavering trust and seamless communication. This bond determined our effectiveness in the field more than any specific skill. My human understood this from the beginning. He treated me not as a tool but as a partner, a companion, a friend.

Our relationship blossomed beyond simple obedience. He understood the subtle nuances of my body language – the tilt of my head, the flick of my tail, the slight shift in my posture – all indicators of my mood, concentration, and understanding. He learned to interpret these signals, to read my emotional state as accurately as he read the wind direction. In return, I learned to read his cues, including his subtle shifts in posture, the tone of his voice, and the slight changes in his breathing, all of which indicated the subtle adjustments needed during a search.

Building trust was not a one-time event but a continuous process, a delicate dance of give and take. It was about consistency, patience, and mutual respect. He never forced me to do anything for which I was not ready. He understood my limitations, both physical and mental, and he constantly adapted his training methods accordingly. If I were tired, he would give me a rest. If I was frustrated, he offered encouragement and reassurance. He never raised his voice, never resorted to punishment. He understood that fear, uncertainty, and stress are counterproductive in a search and rescue operation. A fearful, anxious dog is not an effective search dog.

One particular training exercise stands out. It was a cold, blustery day that chilled you to the bone. We were practicing a grid search in a dense, snow-covered forest. The wind howled through the trees, whipping the snow into swirling vortices. Visibility was poor, and the faint human scent was easily disrupted. I pressed my nose to the ground, straining to separate the scent from the jumble of pine, snow, and damp earth. I faltered, confused, and momentarily lost the trail.

My human did not scold me. He did not display any impatience. He knelt beside me, his warm hand gently stroking my head. His voice, low and reassuring, cut through the howling wind. He spoke softly, almost whispering, his words as soothing as the gentle touch of his hand. He reminded me of the training and the techniques we had practiced, and he reassured me that it was okay to be confused and that it was OK to make mistakes. He then patiently, methodically, and slowly guided me back to the scent trail, tracing the route with his hand to show me the direction, reassuring me with calm words. It was not a quick fix but a demonstration of his unwavering belief in my ability. He showed me that even with the challenges, we faced them together.

It was not his patience and understanding that built our trust; it was also his ability to communicate effectively. He used clear, concise commands, ensuring I understood precisely what was expected. His body language was as important as his voice.

He moved with purpose but also with a calmness that radiated reassurance. Our communication went beyond mere commands; it was a dialogue, a constant exchange of subtle cues and signals. I learned to read his intentions, to anticipate his movements, and to respond accordingly. We became a finely tuned instrument, our actions perfectly synchronized.

Our training sessions were not about learning techniques; they also served as opportunities to strengthen our bond. We played games that enhanced our physical connection and our emotional bond. We spent time at home cuddling, playing fetch, and going for walks. He spoke to me often, not merely issuing commands but engaging me in conversation, sharing details about his day, even when I could not respond. This ongoing interaction fostered companionship, mutual trust, and affection. The confidence he instilled in me was not about believing in my abilities but also about believing in myself. He demonstrated that I could achieve amazing things and overcome obstacles if we worked together. This confidence translated into improved performance. I became more focused, more persistent, more determined. I learned to trust my instincts, to rely on my senses, and to push beyond my perceived limitations.

The bond we shared was a professional partnership and a genuine friendship. This was not a working relationship, but a profound connection that transcended the workplace. It was a connection forged in the crucible of training, strengthened by countless hours spent together in the field and at home. This bond was the key to our success. It gave me the confidence to perform under pressure, persevere through exhaustion, rely on my instincts, and remain focused, even in the most challenging situations.

This mutual trust was essential in challenging searches. One time, we were called to a complicated search—a missing child in a vast, mountainous region. The terrain was treacherous, and the weather was unpredictable. The scent was faint, fragmented, and often carried away by the wind. For hours, we searched, fighting the elements and the constant pull of exhaustion. My body ached, my mind grew weary, and at times I doubted my own abilities.

But then I would catch a glimpse of my human, his steady gaze unwavering, his determination undiminished. His calm demeanor, quiet encouragement, and steadfast belief in me instilled renewed confidence in me. His presence was a source of strength, his trust a lifeline. It was not his physical presence that helped; his calm demeanor was an anchor, his faith in me as a beacon guiding me toward a successful search.

And it was not my confidence that grew. His trust in me also strengthened. He witnessed my abilities, persistence, and unwavering dedication. He saw that I was not a trained animal but a thinking, feeling, capable partner ready to face any challenge alongside him. This confidence, this unbreakable bond, enabled us to achieve things that neither of us could have accomplished individually. We were a team, and our success stemmed from our unwavering trust in one another. The search ended with the successful location of the missing child.

The relief, joy, and sheer exhilaration were more than a professional accomplishment. It was a testament to the power of our partnership, a profound affirmation of the deep connection we shared. Our bond was more than a training exercise; it was the bedrock of our success, a living testament to the transformative power of trust, patience, and understanding. It was the invisible thread that wove together our strengths into a powerful, unstoppable force. The art of the search was not about finding a missing person; it was about finding our way to each other, which proved to be the most incredible discovery of all.

CHAPTER 13
Handling Distractions

The crisp autumn air nipped at my nose as we began our training exercise. The lavender scent trail was meant to guide me to a dummy, symbolizing a missing person. Easy enough, in theory. But theory rarely mirrored reality. This particular training ground bordered a bustling farmer's market. The cacophony of sounds assaulted my sensitive ears – the chatter of vendors, the bleating of sheep from a nearby pen, the excited squeals of children, the rhythmic clang of a blacksmith's hammer, the enticing aroma of roasting nuts and freshly baked bread – a symphony of distractions designed to test my resolve.

My human, sensing my initial hesitation, remained calm, his body language reassuring. He did not push me but patiently waited, allowing me to acclimate to the overwhelming sensory input. He understood that my success did not lie solely in my ability to follow scents but also in my ability to filter out irrelevant information. This was the art of the search—the delicate balance between intense focus and controlled detachment.

Initially, I was overwhelmed. The scent trail, already faint, was further obscured by a potent cocktail of competing aromas – the earthy scent of freshly turned soil, the sweet perfume of flowers, the pungent tang of spices. My nose, usually so sharp and discerning, felt muddled and confused. I veered off course, drawn by the irresistible aroma of freshly baked bread, a scent that triggered primal instincts. My human, sensing my distraction, gently tugged on the lead, a silent correction, a gentle redirection. He did not scold me; his tone remained soft and reassuring, guiding me back to the task and reinforcing the scent I needed to follow.

It was not a quick fix. It was a process of retraining my focus. He used a series of commands and hand signals to guide me back to the lavender scent, which reinforced the idea that this was the most critical smell I needed to focus on. He taught me a new command, "Focus," a single word that became a trigger to shut out all the extraneous stimuli. It was like erecting mental walls around the distracting smells and sounds, blocking them out, allowing me to concentrate solely on the faint lavender trail.

The training continued for weeks, pushing my concentration to its limits. We practiced in increasingly challenging environments: near construction sites teeming with activity, amidst busy street markets, and even near a noisy train station. Each scenario presented a new set of distractions, each a test of my developing ability to filter out irrelevant sensory input and remain locked onto the target scent.

One particular exercise involved a long, winding trail through a dense forest, a trail deliberately designed to evaluate my endurance and concentration. The scent was intentionally faint, and the path was littered with distractions – the tantalizing scent of rabbits, the rustling of squirrels in the undergrowth, the sudden fluttering of a bird, and even the tempting scent of a discarded sausage. I was stretched thin.

Yet, my human's gentle guidance pulled me back with each distraction. His voice, soft yet firm, his touch gentle yet insistent, and his commands concise and clear, continually reinforced the importance of the search. He instilled in me a mental resilience, teaching me to ignore distractions. Slowly and steadily, I learned to ignore the irrelevant, to filter out the noise, and to focus solely on the task at hand. It was not about following a scent but mastering my mind, controlling my impulses, and honing my concentration. It was about mastering self-control.

The improvement was gradual, a testament to the consistency of our training and the unwavering trust we had in each other. The bond we shared was my anchor in the storm of distractions. His calm demeanor, his gentle guidance, his patient reassurance – these were the tools that helped me navigate the maze of sensory overload. His unwavering belief in my abilities instilled in me the confidence I needed to succeed.

We progressed to more complex scenarios, simulating real-life search conditions. We practiced in vast, open fields, where the scent might be carried far and wide, diluted by the wind, interspersed with the smells of livestock and vegetation. We worked in urban areas, navigating bustling streets and crowded spaces, dodging bicycles, cars, and pedestrians. Each scenario was a new challenge, a new test of my ability to filter out the noise and focus on the task at hand.

The success we experienced was not merely a result of technique; it was a testament to our partnership. My human's understanding of my strengths and limitations, his ability to adapt to his training methods accordingly, and his unwavering patience and encouragement were the key ingredients to my success. He never pushed me beyond my limits; he always worked with me, respecting my physical and mental boundaries. He understood that a stressed, overtired dog is not an effective search dog.

During one particularly challenging search, we were tasked with locating a lost hiker in a heavily wooded area. The scent was faint, the terrain rough, and the distractions abundant. The dense forest was filled with a multitude of competing scents—damp earth, decaying leaves, and the smell of wild animals—all vying for my attention. But this time, the ability to block distractions was ingrained in my being.

A flash of bright red startled me, a hiker's jacket discarded carelessly near the trail. My instinct, my untrained self, would have been to investigate. But the training kicked in, the "Focus "command echoing in my mind. I resisted the impulse, pushing the distraction aside, returning my focus to the subtle, almost imperceptible scent of the missing hiker.

The search was long and arduous, but the training paid off. My ability to filter out distractions, combined with my improved sense of smell, enabled me to maintain my focus despite the challenges. We eventually found the hiker, safe and sound, a testament to the power of persistent training and focused attention. It was a moment of profound relief, a confirmation of all the hard work and dedication we had invested in our partnership.

The art of the search was not about finding a missing person; it was about mastering the art of focus, developing the ability to filter out the noise, concentrating on the essential, and ignoring the irrelevant. It was about harnessing the power of concentration and using that power to overcome distractions, persevere through challenges, and achieve our goals. And this was only possible because of the unbreakable bond between handler and dog, a bond built on trust, patience, understanding, and unwavering faith in each other. That was the most significant discovery of all.

CHAPTER 14

Working as a Team

The wind whipped through the tall grass of the training field, carrying with it the faintest trace of eucalyptus- the scent I was tasked with following. This was not any training exercise; it was a simulated rescue scenario designed to evaluate the culmination of months of rigorous training. My human, his face etched with a mixture of anticipation and concern, stood poised, his hand resting lightly on the leash. He knew, as well as I did, that this was a significant test of our teamwork and a testament to the bond we had forged.

The deliberately faint eucalyptus scent was nearly imperceptible among the myriad other smells vying for my attention: the damp earth, decaying leaves, the pungent aroma of wild fennel, and the subtle musk of a nearby deer. This was not merely about detecting a scent; it required a delicate dance of mutual understanding, a seamless collaboration between handler and dog.

My human's body language spoke volumes. He was neither tense nor rigid; instead, his posture was relaxed yet alert, and his movements fluid and subtle. He understood that any sudden, jarring motions could disrupt my concentration and shatter my focus. He subtly guided me, not through forceful tugs on the leash, but with gentle nudges and barely perceptible shifts in his weight- almost imperceptible signals that conveyed trust and encouragement.

The slightest shift in his stance, a barely noticeable tilt of his head toward the direction of the scent, acted as an almost invisible guiding star. His quiet commands, barely a whisper on the wind – "Find it," "Focus," "Good boy" – were delivered with a near-telepathic understanding, perfectly blending encouragement and instruction. They were not barked orders, but relatively soft, gentle whispers, guiding me like a warm breeze.

As I moved through the dense undergrowth, nose twitching and focus unwavering, I felt a deep satisfaction in our collaboration. This was not just about following a scent but about our seamless teamwork, our near-symbiotic connection. My human understood the intricacies of my olfactory world, the subtle nuances of scent, and how I processed information. He knew when to encourage, when to correct, and when to let me work. He was a conductor, guiding my performance with the delicate grace of a maestro.

We encountered a small stream, its rushing water carrying the scent of wet earth and decaying leaves. For a moment, my concentration wavered, drawn to the unusual pungency of the damp leaves. But my human, sensing my hesitation, gave a barely perceptible tug on the leash, a quiet whisper of "Focus," reminding me of the target scent. The gentle tug, a reassuring signal, gently redirected me, realigning me with the path of the eucalyptus scent. It was a silent conversation, a nuanced dialogue between humans and canines, a shared understanding built on mutual respect and trust.

Further on, we encountered a dense thicket of thorny bushes. My natural instinct was to avoid such a barrier. Still, my human gesture—a subtle point in the direction of the thicket, a barely audible encouraging "Go on"—signaled that the scent trail continued through it. He understood that avoiding the obstacle would disrupt my flow, breaking my concentration. His implicit trust in my agility and judgment was reassuring.

We weaved through the thicket, my body pressing against the thorny branches, my scent flowing uninterrupted. I sensed that we were one entity, functioning in perfect harmony, our movements synchronized and our goals unified. It was more than a partnership; it was a dance, a finely choreographed ballet between human and dog, performed with almost supernatural precision and sensitivity. The trust between us was palpable, a silent language that transcended words.

The final stages of the exercise evaluated not only my olfactory abilities but also my capacity to navigate complex terrain. The scent trail led us through a rocky outcrop, requiring me to maneuver along uneven paths and negotiate tricky slopes. My human's guidance was subtle yet crucial. He adjusted his pace to match mine, his movements mirroring my own, and his body language provided constant reassurance. He knew when to encourage, when to offer a reassuring touch, and when to observe and allow me to work independently.

Finally, we reached the dummy representing the lost person, a simulated victim in our rescue scenario. My tail wagged furiously, and my body language expressed a clear "I found them!" My human praised me with quiet enthusiasm, gentle pats, and a soft murmur of affirmation, acknowledging the collaborative effort we'd undertaken. It was not a moment of solo triumph, but a shared accomplishment —a testament to our partnership.

In the coming weeks and months, the simulated rescue scenarios became increasingly complex, each requiring enhanced teamwork and understanding. We trained in urban environments, navigating crowded streets, avoiding obstacles, and dealing with the constant barrage of distracting smells and sounds. We practiced in mountainous regions, maneuvering through dense forests, across swiftly flowing streams, and up steep inclines. Each challenge assessed my physical abilities and the strength and nuance of our collaborative efforts.

We were a team, not a handler and a dog. Individual accomplishments did not measure our success, but by the smooth coordination of our actions, the unspoken communication that flowed between us, and the implicit trust that bound us together. It was a testament to the power of teamwork, the incredible bond between a human and their canine partner. It was the art of the search, honed to perfection through relentless practice and unwavering devotion. And the scent of eucalyptus, once a mere test scent, became a symbol of that collaborative success, a constant reminder of our shared journey and the powerful bond between handler and dog.

CHAPTER 15
Navigating Complex Environments

The transition from the controlled environment of the training field to the unpredictable chaos of the real world was significant. One moment, I navigated a meticulously planned scent trail through neatly arranged obstacles; the next, I was plunged into the heart of a dense, sun-dappled forest, where the air was thick with the scents of pine needles, damp earth, and decaying leaves. The smell I tracked – the faint, lingering trace of a missing hiker – was a whisper compared to the cacophony of smells assaulting my senses. My human, his usual calm demeanor slightly more strained, moved with quiet intensity, his movements carefully calibrated to my progress. He understood the difference between the structured predictability of the training field and the wild card of the real world.

This was about navigating a complex maze of vegetation and deciphering the subtle clues hidden within the forest's tapestry of aromas. The undergrowth was dense, with tangled vines snagging at my paws and branches whipping across my face. I had to engage all my senses, not my nose. My ears strained to pick up the rustle of leaves, the distant call of a bird, and the hushed creak of branches under unseen weight. My human's instructions were fewer and more subtle, relying on almost imperceptible cues – a shift in weight, a barely audible whistle, and a gentle pressure on the leash. He trusted my instincts and my ability to sift through the overwhelming sensory input, focusing on the task at hand.

We encountered a fast-flowing stream, its icy waters cutting a path through the forest floor. The scent I was tracking seemed to vanish, then reappear, faint but persistent, on the other side. My human did not hesitate; he carefully assessed the terrain. He knew I could swim, but he also understood the risk; cold water could disorient me, and the swift current could be dangerous.

Instead of directly plunging into the stream, he guided me upstream, looking for a shallower crossing point. His careful planning and his awareness of my capabilities and limitations underscored the nuanced partnership we had developed. It was not about brute force or relentless pushing, but collaboration, respect, and careful calculation. The success of our search relied not only on my keen sense of smell but also on his strategic thinking and understanding of my strengths and weaknesses. The mountainous terrain presented an entirely different set of challenges. The sheer inclines, the loose scree underfoot, the wind whipping across the exposed ridges – a sensory onslaught.

The scent trail, already faint, was further diluted by the wind, making the search even more arduous. My human, ever vigilant, adjusted his strategy. He slowed our pace, allowing me time to investigate each potential scent marker with meticulous care. He also paid close attention to my body language, interpreting my subtle shifts in posture, the slightest hesitation, and the gentle twitch of my ears. He understood that I was working hard, that this task was demanding, and that even the briefest encouragement could be the difference between success and failure. The thin air, sharp drop-offs, and unpredictable rocky ground necessitated cautious navigation. His constant attention to our safety and my well-being was as crucial as the search itself. This was not a training exercise; it was a dangerous undertaking, a test of my abilities and our collaborative resilience.

The urban environment, with its cacophony of sounds and smells, was the most demanding. The scent trail, this time a lost child, was lost amidst the overwhelming sensory overload: the exhaust fumes of cars, the pungent aroma of street food, the multitude of human scents, the pervasive scent of dogs and other animals. My ability to filter out the irrelevant information and focus solely on the target scent was pushed to its limits. It was akin to sorting through a thousand voices to identify a faint whisper. This was not simply about finding a scent, but about solving a complex puzzle using my keen sense of smell and our shared understanding of the world.

My human adjusted his techniques to match the environment. In the crowded cityscape, he used short bursts of focused searching, punctuated by pauses that gave me time to process the sensory input. Drawing on his knowledge of the streets, he guided me through side alleys, avoided busy intersections, and led me to quieter areas where scents were less chaotic. His understanding of human behavior was as important as his knowledge of canine capabilities. He anticipated crowds, traffic patterns, and potential distractions, constantly adjusting his approach to suit the environment. He was as much a strategist as a handler, his mind working as efficiently and intensely as my nose.

One particularly challenging search led us through a bustling marketplace, a cacophony of sights, sounds, and smells. My human, navigating through the throngs of people, subtly guided me through the labyrinthine stalls, his body language as deft as a dancer's. He used hand signals and barely audible commands, weaving through the crowded space with an almost supernatural awareness. He never lost focus or sight of our objective. We were a team, functioning in perfect harmony, a seamless blend of canine intuition and human strategic thinking. The trust between us was absolute, an unspoken understanding that transcended words.

Our successes were not about finding the missing person; they were about the perfect synergy between my abilities and his experience, insight, planning, and my instincts. Each search was a lesson, a refinement of our teamwork, a testament to the strength of our bond. The complex environments, far from being obstacles, became opportunities for us to evaluate our limits, hone our skills, and deepen our understanding of each other.

With every search, we learned to adapt, evolve, and become a more efficient and effective team. The scent of eucalyptus, initially used as a training aid, had now become a symbolic reminder of our journey —a symbol of our shared successes and unwavering teamwork.

These challenging experiences cemented our bond, forging a partnership built on mutual respect, trust, and unwavering reliance. It was not about obedience or skill; it was about the unspoken language of collaboration, the shared understanding that bound us together in the face of adversity. The silent conversation, the intuitive cooperation, and the seamless integration of our strengths and abilities defined our success. It was the art of the search, perfected not in a controlled setting but in the unpredictable, often chaotic, reality of the world around us. And it was, above all, a story of unwavering devotion, of a dog and his human, working together, not as partners, but as a single, unified entity, dedicated to finding those who were lost. Each challenging environment and seemingly insurmountable obstacle only strengthened our bond and refined our collaborative prowess, making us a stronger, more effective team.

CHAPTER 16
The First Real Mission

The crackle of the radio broke the tense silence in the jeep. My human, his face etched with a grim determination, adjusted the headset. The voice on the other end, crackling with static, relayed the details: a young boy, lost in the Redwood National Park, missing for over twelve hours. The urgency in their voice sent a shiver down my spine, a prickling sensation that went beyond the cool night air. This was not a training exercise; this was real. This was life or death.

The familiar scent of eucalyptus, the marker we used in training, hung faintly in the air, starkly contrasting the earthy, damp smell of the redwood forest that now enveloped us. The transition from the controlled environment of the training field to this wild, unpredictable wilderness was jarring. The scent trails we would practice were precise and methodical; this was a complex tapestry woven from the scent of damp earth, decaying leaves, pine needles, and the faint, elusive trace of a child.

The jeep lurched forward, the tires crunching on the gravel road. My human, usually so calm and collected, was noticeably tense. His hand rested lightly on my head, a silent reassurance, a subtle gesture that spoke volumes. He was not my handler; he was my partner, protector, and friend. We were a team, and at this moment, the weight of that responsibility pressed down on us both.

As we ventured deeper into the park, the towering redwoods cast long, eerie shadows, transforming the familiar landscape into a beautiful and menacing place. The air grew colder, and the silence was punctuated only by the rustling of leaves and the occasional snap of a twig underfoot. My nose, my most trusted tool, worked tirelessly, sifting through the scents, searching for the faintest hint of the missing boy.

The initial search was frustrating. The boy's scent was faint, almost imperceptible, masked by the overwhelming smells of the forest. I worked tirelessly, my nose to the ground, my body low to the earth, my tail held low, a testament to the seriousness of the task. My ever-watchful human moved with quiet precision, his movements guided by my progress, his eyes constantly scanning the surroundings. He was my anchor in this chaotic sea of scents, a constant presence that provided security in a place that felt alien and unsettling.

We searched for hours, the moon casting long, dancing shadows that played tricks on my eyes. The forest's silence was broken only by the rhythmic beat of my paws on the forest floor and my human's hushed whispers of encouragement. His quiet confidence was contagious, calming my growing anxiety. The weight of responsibility pressed heavily on my young shoulders as I understood that life could depend on my success. It was not about finding a scent but saving a life.

As the night wore on, fatigue threatened to cloud my senses. The forest, once a familiar training ground, now felt vast and menacing, filled with hidden dangers and potential pitfalls. But my human's unwavering support and his constant reassurance kept me going. He knew when to push me, when to give me rest, and when to offer a gentle word of encouragement. Our connection was a partnership built on mutual trust, respect, and a shared understanding of our immense responsibility.

Then, a breakthrough. A faint but unmistakable scent, a whisper against the cacophony of the forest smells. It was faint and fleeting, yet unmistakably the scent of a child —a unique blend of sweat, earth, and the subtle aroma of his belongings. My tail, previously low and subdued, began to wag slightly, a silent acknowledgment of the discovery. My pace quickened; my body language shifted, signaling to my human that I had found a lead.

The scent led us through dense undergrowth, past towering redwoods that seemed to watch our every move. The path was treacherous, the ground uneven, and my human navigated it with incredible caution, always mindful of my safety. He was not only tracking a lost child; he was meticulously protecting me, ensuring I could focus on the task ahead. We moved as one, a perfectly coordinated dance of human intelligence and canine instinct.

Finally, we reached a small clearing. There, huddled beneath a giant redwood, was the boy. He looked up, his eyes wide with relief, his small body trembling with exhaustion and fear. Seeing him triggered an explosion of emotion – relief, joy, and a profound sense of accomplishment washed over me. It was more than just finding a scent; it was the culmination of months of rigorous training, the unwavering dedication of my human, and the powerful bond that had formed between us.

The reunion was emotional, a powerful reminder of the impact our work had on the lives we touched. The boy's parents, their faces streaked with tears, rushed towards him, embracing him in a tight hug. Their relief was palpable, a wave of emotion that washed over me, reaffirming the purpose and significance of our mission.

The drive back was quiet, as exhaustion began to set in. But the silence was filled with a different weight – the weight of success, the quiet satisfaction of a job well done, the profound understanding of the responsibility we both shouldered. It was not about finding a lost child; it was about saving a life, strengthening our bond, and demonstrating the power of partnership between humans and dogs. The scent of eucalyptus, a reminder of our training, no longer felt like a training aid but a symbol of our shared victory —a testament to the extraordinary bond we had forged in the heart of the Redwood Forest. It was the beginning of a journey, a testament to our shared devotion, and an affirmation of the profound responsibility and the immense reward of being a search and rescue team.

CHAPTER 17
Facing Fear and Uncertainty

The adrenaline rush faded, leaving behind a hollow ache in my chest. The boy was safe, and his family reunited, but the echoes of the forest, the chilling silence punctuated only by the frantic beating of my own heart, lingered. My human, usually a pillar of calm, sat beside me, his hand resting on my flank, his breath coming in ragged gasps. He did not speak, but his trembling hand betrayed the depth of emotion he was struggling to contain.

The relentless pressure of the search, the sheer weight of responsibility, had squeezed the air from my lungs. I had felt it – a profound, almost overwhelming fear. It was not the fear of the dark, the shadows, or the unfamiliar sounds of the night. It was the fear of failure, the chilling thought that my nose, my finely-tuned instinct, might fail me. The image of that lost boy, his face etched with terror, haunted me.

My human understood. He knew the silent language of fear, the subtle shifts in my body language, the tremor in my breath. He did not scold or pressure me; instead, he spoke softly, his voice a soothing, calming against the lingering fear. He ran his fingers through my fur, a gesture of comfort, a silent affirmation of our shared experience. He knew I had given my all and pushed myself to the limits of my abilities, and that was enough.

That night, curled up beside him in the warmth of the jeep, sleep eluded me. In my dreams, the forest transformed into a maze of shadows, and the scent of the boy lingered as a fleeting whisper amid the overwhelming cacophony of other smells. I relived moments of uncertainty, feeling the creeping doubt that threatened to consume me and the fear that I might not be good enough.

The following days were a blur of debriefings, meetings, and well-deserved rest. However, the experience left an indelible mark. The weight of responsibility, once a distant concept, had become tangible-a constant companion, a reminder of the life-or-death stakes involved in our work. It made me question my abilities, resilience, and the extent of my capabilities.

My human sensed this change in me. He did not dismiss my anxieties but addressed them with patience and understanding. He explained that fear was not a weakness, but a natural response to danger- a vital survival instinct. He emphasized the importance of acknowledging and managing fear rather than suppressing it. He taught me coping mechanisms, breathing exercises, and techniques to ground myself in the present moment, allowing me to focus on the task at hand instead of the overwhelming potential consequences.

We started small, revisiting familiar training grounds and carefully rebuilding my confidence. The controlled environment and predictable scents helped to ease my anxieties. He introduced new techniques, focusing on building resilience and increasing my ability to manage pressure. We practiced in increasingly challenging scenarios, gradually pushing my boundaries while ensuring my safety and comfort at all times.

He admitted that the responsibility for another person's life was immense and that he, too, felt the pressure, uncertainty, and fear of failure. This honesty was unexpected and deeply comforting. It reminded me that we were both vulnerable, both capable of fear, and both dedicated to overcoming challenges.

Our bond deepened; it was no longer about obedience and commands, but about mutual support, shared understanding, and unwavering trust. We became a team, intertwined in our shared purpose, anxieties, and triumphs. He became not only my handler but also my confidant, mentor, and friend.

The next mission arrived sooner than expected: a hiker had lost his way in the mountains, his location uncertain, and his condition unknown. This time, I approached the challenge with a newfound perspective. The fear was still there, a nagging voice in the back of my mind, but it was tempered by the confidence gained from our training and by the strength of our bond.

The mountain air was crisp, with the scent of pine and damp earth filling my nostrils. My nose worked tirelessly, sifting through the intricate tapestry of smells and searching for the faintest trace of the missing hiker. Now and then, the scent would fade, bringing back the uncertainty and prompting that familiar pang of fear. But this time, I had the tools to combat it. I focused on my breathing, grounding myself in the present, trusting my instincts, and relying on my human's guidance.

My human, too, seemed calmer and more confident. He read my body language with a sensitivity I had not noticed before. When my pace slowed, he offered gentle encouragement; when I hesitated, he provided reassurance. He was not watching for my signals; he was attuned to my emotions, interpreting the subtle cues that betrayed my anxiety. We communicated not through words and commands but through a silent, unspoken language that transcended words.

The search was challenging but ultimately successful. We found the hiker, tired but unharmed. The relief that washed over me was immense, as was the sense of accomplishment. I conquered my fear and showcased resilience, determination, and the strength of my partnership with my human.

Back in the jeep, heading home, the silence was not one of exhaustion but of quiet contemplation. The weight of responsibility still lingered, yet it felt different. It was no longer a burden, but a challenge —a shared commitment that strengthened our bond. The fear remained, serving as a poignant reminder of the risks we had taken, but it was now a manageable companion-a testament to our resilience and a mark of our shared courage.

We continued our work; each mission was a new test, and each success served as a testament to our growth. The fear never completely disappeared, but it ceased to be debilitating. It evolved into a subtle undercurrent, reminding us of the magnitude of our work, acting as a catalyst for perseverance, and illustrating the power of our shared journey. We learned to confront uncertainty together, with our partnership forged in the crucible of fear and reflecting the powerful bond between a dog and his human, founded not only on obedience and training but also on shared trust, mutual respect, and unwavering commitment. Although the weight of responsibility remained, we now bore it together.

CHAPTER 18
Working Under Pressure

The next search was different. It was not the sprawling wilderness we were accustomed to but the claustrophobic confines of a collapsed building. The air hung heavy with the scent of dust and debris, a thick, suffocating blanket that clung to my fur and filled my nostrils. The rhythmic thump-thump-thump of the rescue workers' boots echoed through the wreckage, a counterpoint to the frantic whispers of hope and fear that hung in the air. This was not a forest; this was a maze of splintered wood, twisted metal, and crushing silence, broken only by the occasional groan of the unstable structure.

My human's hand was firm on my harness, his presence a reassuring anchor in the chaos. The pressure was intense. The scent of the missing person—a young woman trapped beneath the rubble—was faint, intermittent, almost lost within the overpowering smells of destruction. Doubt, that insidious serpent coiled in the pit of my stomach. Could I find her? Would my nose be sharp enough, my instincts strong enough to pierce through the overwhelming olfactory confusion?

The fear was not a distant whisper this time; it was a roaring torrent threatening to pull me under. My breath came in short, shallow gasps; my muscles tensed. I could feel the panic rising, a wave threatening to crash over me and drown my concentration. But I remembered my training. I focused on my breath, the slow, deliberate inhales and exhales that my human had taught me. I felt the familiar rhythm grounding me, anchoring me to the present moment, pulling me back from the precipice of panic.

I pushed forward, inching through the narrow gaps, my body a symphony of controlled movement. My nose worked tirelessly, a finely tuned instrument sifting through the cacophony of smells. The scent of the young woman was elusive, a fleeting phantom that appeared and disappeared, teasing me and evaluating my resolve. But I persevered, my focus unwavering, my determination fueled by the knowledge that someone's life depended on me.

My human, sensing my struggle, whispered words of encouragement, his voice calm in the storm. He did not push me; he guided me, his touch gentle but firm, his words a beacon in the darkness. He understood the subtle shifts in my body language, the tremor in my breath, the slight hesitation in my gait. He knew when to encourage and when to reassure, when to push, and when to pull back. He was my anchor, partner, and unwavering support in the face of overwhelming pressure.

The scent grew stronger, more defined. I followed it, my body weaving through the debris, my nose glued to the ground. Then, I found her. She was trapped, injured, but alive. The relief that washed over me was indescribable. The fear receded, replaced by an overwhelming surge of elation. I had done it. I had found her.

The rescue workers swarmed around us; their faces etched with relief. The weight of responsibility, once a crushing burden, now felt lighter, replaced by a profound sense of accomplishment. I had performed under immense pressure, maintained my focus, and ultimately succeeded. All our training, trust, and bond had led to this triumph.

Later, back in the jeep's calm, the adrenaline faded, leaving behind a deep sense of exhaustion but also a profound satisfaction. I had faced my fears, conquered my doubts, and proven my capabilities. The experience had etched itself into my memory, not as a source of trauma but as a testament to my resilience and the power of training and partnership.

The following weeks were filled with more searches, each one a unique challenge and a test of my abilities and our bond. We worked in varied environments, facing different obstacles and encountering unpredictable circumstances. But through it all, the lessons learned in the collapsed building remained imprinted on my mind. I learned to manage my fear, trust my instincts, and rely on my human's guidance. We developed a deeper understanding, a silent language of trust and support that transcended words.

One mission took us to a vast, desolate desert. The sun beat down mercilessly, radiating heat from the parched earth, turning the air into a shimmering haze. The scent of the missing person—an elderly woman with dementia—was faint, almost nonexistent, lost within the vastness of the landscape. Pressure mounted, not from the heat and exhaustion but from the sheer immensity of the search area. The fear crept back, whispering doubts and questioning my abilities.

But I drew strength from our shared experiences. I remembered the collapsed building, the frantic whispers, the overwhelming pressure, and how we had overcome it together. I focused on my breath, the rhythm grounding me, my human's reassuring presence a constant support. We worked as one, our movements synchronized, our minds attuned to each other.

The search was long, arduous, and emotionally draining. The landscape was unforgiving, the sun merciless, and hope dwindled with each passing hour. But we persevered, driven by our shared determination. Finally, after what seemed like an eternity, we found her. She was weak and disoriented but alive. The relief was profound, the joy overwhelming. We had done it again.

The journey back was quiet, the setting sun painting the desert sky in hues of orange and purple. The weight of responsibility remained, but it no longer felt like a crushing burden. It was a testament to our partnership.

The fear had been tamed, transformed into a drive for perseverance, a reminder of the importance of our work and the strength of our bond. With each mission, our shared experience grew, and each success reinforced our partnership. The pressure never fully disappeared, but we learned to navigate it together, embrace the challenges, trust our instincts, and rely on one another's strength.

CHAPTER 19
The Thrill of Success

The jeep rattled along the bumpy forest track, the familiar scent of pine and damp earth filling my nostrils. The adrenaline was fading, leaving behind a pleasant exhaustion that settled deep in my muscles. My human, his face etched with relief and quiet pride, reached down and scratched behind my ears. The simple gesture was a calming, silent acknowledgment of our shared triumph. We had found her. The little girl, lost for hours in the dense woods, was safe.

The memory of her scent, initially faint and elusive, then growing stronger as I tracked her through the undergrowth, was still sharp in my mind. It was a complex scent, a blend of fear and sweat, mixed with the subtle tang of her candy bar wrapper—a detail my human had relayed to me before the search. Following that faint trail, weaving through the tangled branches and thorny bushes, had been a test of my endurance and my skill. The pressure had been immense, but the determination to succeed had pushed me forward.

Finding her had not been a sudden, dramatic revelation. There was no triumphant bark, no joyous leap. It was more subtle, a quiet certainty that settled in my bones. I had sniffed the air, my nose to the ground, until I detected the telltale signs of her presence – the faintest trace of her scent against the decaying leaves. She was huddled beneath a thicket of ferns, her small form hidden from view, her whimpers barely audible above the rustling leaves. When I nudged her gently with my nose, her small hand reached out, her touch surprisingly strong.

The relief surging through me was more powerful than any emotion I had experienced. It was not the satisfaction of a job well done; it was a profound wave of joy and accomplishment, a feeling of deep satisfaction that went beyond the physical act of the search. It was the culmination of months of training, countless hours spent honing my skills, the unwavering trust my human had placed in me, and the bond we had forged through shared challenges and triumphs. It was the realization that we were more than a dog and his handler; we were a team, a partnership forged in mutual respect and a shared purpose.

My human, equally relieved, knelt beside her, his voice soft and reassuring as he checked for injuries. The little girl, initially hesitant, soon nestled against him, her small body trembling with exhaustion and relief. The sight of their embrace filled me with a quiet warmth, satisfaction that transcended the excitement of the successful rescue. I had played a vital role in reuniting them, and that knowledge filled me with a deep sense of purpose.

The journey back to the base was filled with quiet satisfaction. My human did not speak much; he stroked my fur occasionally, his hand resting on my head, a silent communication of appreciation and shared accomplishment. The team greeted us with cheers and heartfelt congratulations, their relief palpable. Though sincere, their words were secondary to the silent understanding between my human and me, a language of shared accomplishment and deep trust.

That night, curled up at the foot of my human's bed, the day's events replayed in my mind. The fear, the doubt, the intense pressure of the search—all of it receded into the background, overshadowed by the overwhelming joy of success. It was not the thrill of the chase or the satisfaction of finding the missing person; it was something deeper —a profound sense of fulfillment that stemmed from knowing I had made a real difference in someone's life. It was the feeling of having lived up to the trust placed in me, the satisfaction of knowing I had played a crucial role in a happy ending.

The following days were a blur of routine checks, tail wags, and the comforting scent of my human's familiar clothes. The intensity of the search had waned, giving way to quiet contentment. But the memory of the little girl's relieved smile, the warmth of my human's touch, and the deep sense of accomplishment remained. It was a potent cocktail of emotions, a potent reminder of the powerful bond between a dog and his human, and the extraordinary things we could achieve together.

The feeling of fulfillment, however, was not solely mine. My human felt it, too, though expressed differently. While I experienced it as a physical warmth and a deep-seated contentment, he carried it as quiet pride and a renewed sense of purpose. I saw it in his eyes, the soft smile playing on his lips, as he spoke about the rescue, his voice filled with deep satisfaction. It was a shared accomplishment, a testament to our bond and unwavering dedication to our shared task.

One evening, after a particularly successful week in which we had located three missing hikers, he sat beside me, quietly petting my fur. The fire crackled softly in the hearth, casting dancing shadows on the walls. He spoke then, not of technical details of the searches, but of the pure emotion, the overwhelming sense of relief, and the profound joy of seeing the reunited families. He spoke of the human element, the weight of responsibility lifted, the shared burden eased by the successful missions. His words, though few, resonated deeply. They were not instructions, commands, or critiques of my performance, but rather a heartfelt appreciation —an unspoken acknowledgment of our partnership and the success we had achieved together.

The thrill of success was not merely a fleeting moment; it became a powerful motivator for further achievement. While still fraught with challenges and anxieties, each subsequent search was fueled by the memory of that profound satisfaction. The weight of responsibility remained a constant undercurrent in our work. Still, it was now counterbalanced by the knowledge that we possessed the skills, the training, and the bond to overcome adversity and succeed. We were a team, capable of achieving extraordinary things, bound together by more than a shared purpose; we were connected by a deep, abiding mutual respect and trust.

The following months continued to bring their fair share of challenges. A search in a blizzard, a grueling search in a dense forest at night, and the heartbreaking cases where we could not locate the missing persons. Even in those instances, the memories of successful missions fueled our resolve. We had learned from our mistakes. We had learned the importance of perseverance, the resilience from a strong bond, and the unwavering trust that transcends words.

In the quieter moments between missions, nestled by the fireside, I often felt the warmth of my human's hand on my head. These were unspoken moments of shared experience, shared successes and failures, shared anxieties and triumphs. They were the moments that deepened our bond, strengthened our resolve, and reminded us of the profound and life-affirming nature of our work. The thrill of success, therefore, was not a fleeting feeling but a constant source of motivation—a testament to our enduring partnership and a potent reminder of the incredible bond between a dog and its owner. It was a bond forged in trust, tempered by challenges, and strengthened by shared victories. It was, in essence, the heart of our work, the foundation of our success, and the source of our enduring happiness. And that, I knew, was worth more than any reward.

CHAPTER 20
The Burden of Failure

The biting wind whipped around us, stinging my eyes and making my fur stand on end. The scent of snow, sharp and clean, filled the air, but it offered no solace. The scent I sought, the faintest whisper of human life, was gone, swallowed by the vast, unforgiving wilderness. Three days. For three days, we scoured the snow-covered mountains, following every faint clue, yet found nothing.

The silence after the official call-off was deafening. My human, usually brimming with energy and purpose, was quiet, his shoulders slumped, his usual bright eyes clouded with a weariness that went beyond physical exhaustion. He did not speak or even pat me as he usually did after a search, successful or not. The absence of his touch and the lack of his usual reassuring words spoke volumes. I sensed his disappointment, his frustration, his gnawing self-doubt. It mirrored my internal turmoil; the unspoken weight of failure pressed down on us both.

The jeep ride back was torturous. The familiar bumps in the road felt jarring, and the silence amplified the weight of our shared disappointment. The team's usual camaraderie was replaced by a subdued quiet, a collective feeling of frustration and helplessness. Their sympathetic glances towards my human, their muted words of encouragement, were insufficient to ease the heavy atmosphere.

Each sympathetic pat on my head felt like an acknowledgment of shared failure, a heavy reminder of our inability to bring the missing hiker home.

Curled at the foot of his bed that night, I felt the familiar weight of his hand on my head, but it lacked its usual comforting warmth. It was a heavy hand, a hand burdened by the weight of his responsibility, his failure. The soothing scent of his skin, usually laced with the familiar scents of pine and wood smoke, was tinged with the sharp scent of his suppressed grief. I nudged his hand, seeking comfort, but my usually enthusiastic attempts at solace seemed futile. His sighs were deep and heavy, each with a tremor that reverberated through the silent room, a testament to the emotional toll of the failed mission.

The days that followed were a blur of muted routines, a stark contrast to the vibrant activity that usually characterized our lives. The training exercises felt hollow; a heavy disillusionment replaced the usual enthusiasm. The commands felt perfunctory; my responses, which were typically precise and enthusiastic, had now become lackluster, mirroring his somber mood. The familiar joy in our daily routines was replaced by a heavy silence that seemed to hang in the air, weighing down every interaction.

I knew, somehow, that my human blamed himself. He had pored over the maps repeatedly, retracing our steps, analyzing every decision made, every scent followed, every choice that led us astray. He doubted his judgment, ability, and instincts—all aspects of his confidence collapsed due to this failure. I sensed his struggle, his internal battle against self-doubt. It was a subtle battle fought in silence, marked by heavy sighs, sleepless nights, and the absence of his customary boisterous energy. The silent struggle echoed within me; I felt the sting of failure acutely, as if the weight of his disappointment were also mine to bear.

The unspoken burden hung between us, a tangible thing that affected everything. The usual lightness in our interactions was gone. His usual playful banter was replaced by a serious reserve, his interactions with me lacking the familiar warmth and spontaneity. The routine tasks, which usually brought us both purpose and fulfillment, felt hollow; the energy had drained from them, leaving emptiness and frustration. The failure had cast a shadow over our lives, permeating every aspect of our shared existence.

In those moments of quiet despair, I realized the actual depth of our bond. It was not about the successes, the triumphant rescues, the joyous reunions. It was about the shared burden, disappointments, and resilience in the face of adversity. Our partnership extended beyond the thrill of a successful search; it encompassed the darkness of failure and the crushing weight of responsibility when our efforts fell short. The silent moments spent by the hearth, the shared weight of our unspoken grief, forged an even deeper connection, a bond tempered by adversity, strengthened by shared struggles.

Slowly, we emerged from the shadow of that failure. Healing came not in grand gestures but in quiet moments, a shared gaze, the comfort of his touch, and the silent acknowledgment of our bond rekindled through small acts of connection.

The next search was a different experience. The weight of the previous failure hung heavily, but it was different; it was no longer crippling. The anxiety was still present, but it was tempered by a growing resilience and a learned acceptance of the inherent risks and uncertainties associated with our work. We had faced our failure and emerged stronger; our bond forged anew in the crucible of shared disappointment.

It was not a forgetting of the past but an acceptance of the reality of our work. There would be successes and failures, moments of triumph, and moments of deep sorrow. But it was through confronting these moments, embracing the uncertainties, and learning from our mistakes that our strength would deepen, our partnership would endure, and our purpose would remain steadfast. The burden of failure, once overwhelming, became a part of our shared narrative—a reminder of the profound weight of responsibility and the remarkable resilience of the bond between a dog and its owner.

The weight of responsibility remained, but now it was a shared weight, carried not with despair but with the quiet strength born of shared experience and unshakeable mutual trust.

CHAPTER 21

The Unbreakable Link

The wind had shifted, carrying a different scent now – the sharp tang of pine and damp earth, a comforting familiarity after the sterile, icy smell of the previous search. We were back in our familiar training grounds, the sprawling expanse of the forest, a welcome change from the stark, unforgiving mountains. But even here, amidst the comforting routine, the shadow of our failure lingered. My human moved through the exercises with quiet intensity, his usual exuberance muted; his commands were precise but lacked their usual cheerful inflection.

I mirrored his mood. The agility course, usually a joyous dance of leaps and bounds, felt mechanical, the familiar sequence of jumps and tunnels executed with a precision born of habit rather than enthusiasm. The scent work, usually a thrilling game of hide-and-seek, lacked its usual zest. Even the simple act of fetching the dummy felt different, devoid of the usual joyful exuberance. The shared silence following the failed search had woven itself into the fabric of our days, a quiet undercurrent that permeated every interaction.

He was emotionally drained. I could sense it in how he held himself, in the quiet intensity of his gaze, in the subtle tightening of his jaw. He had always been my rock, my unwavering guide, the source of my steadfast confidence. But now, I sensed a fragility beneath his stoic exterior, a vulnerability that touched me profoundly.

One evening, after a particularly grueling training session, he sat by the fire, his usual cheerful demeanor replaced by a pensive quiet. He did not speak, stared into the flames, his face etched with a weariness that went beyond mere fatigue. I nudged his hand with my nose, seeking to offer comfort, my usual playful nudges tinged with a newfound empathy. He looked down at me, a flicker of something – sadness, perhaps, or maybe exhaustion – in his eyes. He scratched behind my ears, the familiar gesture laced with a tenderness that was both familiar and newly poignant.

The silence was not uncomfortable; it was a shared silence, a silent acknowledgment of our mutual disappointment, a tacit understanding of the weight we both carried. It was in this shared silence that I came to understand the depth of our bond. It was not a bond built solely on triumphs and celebrations; it was a bond forged in the crucible of shared experience, strengthened by our shared struggles and disappointments. It was a bond that transcended words, expressed through shared gazes, comforting touches, and the quiet understanding that flowed between us.

His training methods have changed subtly. He was not shouting commands; he was whispering encouragement, his voice soft and reassuring. His touch was gentler, his patience boundless. He seemed to understand that my lack of enthusiasm was not a lack of ability but a reflection of his emotional state. He was not training a dog but nurturing a relationship, rebuilding our shared confidence, brick by brick.

One day, he brought a new toy, a worn, floppy stuffed animal. It was not the high-tech training equipment we usually used; instead, it was something soft and straightforward that conveyed comfort and reassurance. He threw it for me, a simple act yet profoundly meaningful. It was a gesture of playfulness, a return to the simpler joys of our early days together, a conscious effort to rebuild our connection on a foundational level.

He started taking me on shorter, less demanding searches, focusing on building our confidence and honing our skills in a less pressured environment. We practiced tracking in the familiar woods, searching for scents in the familiar undergrowth. The successes were small—finding a hidden toy, tracing a familiar scent—but each success, however small, built our confidence, reinforcing our connection. Each successful find was a small victory, a building block in our journey back to complete working order.

The renewed training was not about skills; it was about rebuilding our shared trust. It reminded us of our strength, resilience, and unwavering partnership. It was a reminder that our bond remained unbreakable even in the face of failure. It was a quiet affirmation of our mutual respect and love, expressed through shared breaths, shared glances, and the silent language of companionship.

The next time we were called to a search, the atmosphere was different. The weight of the previous failure remained, but it did not cripple us. The anxiety was still there, a familiar companion, but it was tempered by the newfound resilience we had cultivated. We searched with calm determination, and our actions were precise and purposeful. We worked as one, each movement reflecting the other, a seamless dance of mutual understanding and unwavering trust.

The scent was faint, almost imperceptible, but I managed to catch it. A faint whisper of human life carried on the wind. I followed it, my human close behind, his hand resting gently on my back, a reassuring presence that guided me through the dense undergrowth. We found her nestled beneath a thicket of bushes, weak but alive. The relief was palpable, washing over me in an intense wave of emotion. But it was not the relief of the rescue; it was the relief of a shared victory, a testament to the resilience of our bond, a reaffirmation of our shared purpose.

The usual camaraderie was present, but it felt different, deeper. It was infused with a shared understanding, an acknowledgment of our shared journey, our shared struggles, and our shared triumphs. My human's hug was tighter, his words softer, filled with an overwhelming gratitude and relief that went beyond the mission's success. It was a moment of profound connection, an acknowledgment of the unbreakable link forged in the training grounds and the crucible of shared disappointment and triumphant success.

In the quiet moments that followed, curled up at his feet, the warmth of his hand on my head was more profound than ever. The weight of responsibility remained, but now it was a weight we shared—a shared burden carried with quiet strength—a shared burden that only served to strengthen the unbreakable link that bound us together. It was not a partnership, but a bond forged in fire, tempered by adversity, and strengthened by the unwavering trust and mutual respect that defined our unique and unbreakable connection. The scent of pine and wood smoke filled the air, a comforting reminder of our shared journey, purpose, and the unbreakable bond that connected us.

CHAPTER 22

Communication Beyond Words

The crisp autumn air nipped at my nose, a welcome contrast to the sweat still clinging to my fur after our morning training session. My human, still flushed from exertion, tossed a worn tennis ball. It was not a particularly exciting fetch; the ball was old, its fuzzy surface matted and faded. Yet, the simple act held a significance beyond the game itself. It was a bridge, a gentle return to the lightheartedness that had seemed to evaporate in the wake of our recent failure. I retrieved the ball, my tail wagging not out of mere obedience but out of a more profound understanding – a silent acknowledgment of his attempt to reconnect, to rebuild the rhythm of our shared days.

He did not throw the ball; he observed. He watched the subtle shift in my weight as I anticipated his throw, the twitch of my ears as I tracked its trajectory, the precision of my leap. He did not need words to understand my readiness, my eagerness to please. He understood the silent language of my body – the way my tail held itself, the slight tilt of my head, the intensity of my focus. It was not a scientific analysis, but an intuitive understanding —a deeply ingrained connection forged through months of shared experiences. These were not training sessions, but conversations conducted without a single word.

Later, while he prepared dinner, I lay at his feet, watching him. The subtle movements of his hands, the way he hummed a soft tune as he chopped vegetables, the quiet sigh of contentment as he leaned back against the counter – were details I absorbed, not as separate occurrences but as threads woven into the rich tapestry of our understanding. He looked down, his gaze lingering on me momentarily, a silent acknowledgment of our shared space, our unspoken bond. It was not a stare, but a connection —a shared understanding that transcended words. In those shared moments, I felt a kinship, an intimacy born not from physical touch but from a deeper, more profound connection.

Our communication was a symphony of subtle cues, a dance of unspoken understanding. A slight change in his posture, the way he

held his hands, the subtle shift in his gaze – these messages reached me far more profoundly than any spoken command. I understood the subtle tightening of his jaw as he prepared for a critical maneuver during a search, and the way his shoulders relaxed when he found a scent trail. These nonverbal signals formed the foundation of our shared understanding, creating a language that was more nuanced, profound, and infinitely sensitive than any human language could be.

He did not need to yell, "Find!" for me to understand the urgency of the search. A simple tightening of his grip on the leash, a slight increase in the pace of his steps, the barely perceptible shift in his body weight—these were enough. It was a delicate dance of unspoken communication, a subtle interplay of energy that flowed between us with seamless and effortless ease. I responded not to his commands but to his intentions, his emotional state, and the subtle undercurrents of his thoughts.

During a particularly rigorous training session, I sensed his frustration mounting one evening. He was struggling with a specific maneuver, and his movements were tense and clumsy. He stopped, his shoulders slumped in exhaustion, frustration etched on his face. I approached him cautiously, nudging his hand with my nose, my tail wagging slowly, offering comfort rather than playful exuberance. He looked down at me, a quiet sadness in his eyes, and instead of continuing the exercise, he sat beside me, his hand gently resting on my head. That shared silence was more meaningful than any words could have been.

Our communication was not limited to the training grounds. It was an ongoing dialogue of subtle gestures and shared moments at home. A gentle scratch behind my ears, a quiet hum as he read, a shared nap on the rug, the comforting weight of his hand resting on my back – these weren't isolated acts but parts of a continuous conversation, a rich tapestry of unspoken understanding that formed the foundation of our relationship.

I learned to read him as well as I read scents. I knew when he was happy – the way his eyes sparkled, the lightness in his step, the infectious cheerfulness in his voice. And I knew when he was worried – the slight frown, the tightening of his lips, the way he repeatedly checked his watch. These were not intentional signals; they were involuntary expressions of his inner state, and I learned to understand them as well as the language of wind and earth.

He, in turn, learned to read my moods. He knew when I was tired –the way I slowed my pace, the drooping of my ears. He knew when I was excited – the frantic wagging of my tail, the bright gleam in my eyes, the eager bouncing on my feet. He understood that my silence was not always an absence of understanding, but sometimes a sign of concentration —a sign of my focused attention. It was a mutual understanding, a silent dialogue where each gesture, each expression, and each shared moment spoke volumes.

Our bond was not merely a human-animal relationship, but a profound connection founded on mutual respect, trust, and an unspoken language that transcended words. It was a silent symphony of shared emotions, experiences, and aspirations, played out in the subtle nuances of body language, the comforting weight of a hand, and the quiet understanding that passed between us in the shared silences. And it was this invisible thread, this unspoken understanding, that strengthened our bond, forging a connection that was as resilient as it was profound. It was a connection that would prove invaluable in the demanding world of search and rescue, as well as in every shared moment of our lives. It was, in its essence, the heart of our partnership.

CHAPTER 23

Shared Triumphs and Setbacks

The biting wind whipped around us as we navigated the treacherous terrain of the mountainside. The faint but persistent scent clung to the icy air—the trace of a missing hiker. My human, his face grim with determination, tightened his grip on my leash. This was not a training exercise; this was real. This was life or death. The pressure was palpable, a tangible weight pressing down on us.

For weeks, the scent had eluded us. We had scoured the valley, the forests, every conceivable pathway, but to no avail. The exhaustion was evident in his slumped shoulders, in the lines etched deep into his brow. Yet, he never faltered, his unwavering resolve a beacon in the face of adversity. He was my rock, my anchor in the storm of uncertainty. And I, in turn, was his unwavering companion, my nose to the ground, my senses acutely attuned to the subtle whispers of the wind.

This search felt different. The air itself seemed to hum with foreboding. The usual confidence that fueled our teamwork faltered. Doubt, that insidious serpent, began to coil in my human's heart; I could sense it. It was not a verbal expression but a subtle shift in his body language – a slight hesitation in his step, a tightening in his jaw, a flicker of doubt in his eyes. I pressed closer, nudging his hand with my wet nose, offering him the silent reassurance only a loyal companion could provide. We pressed on, the wind howling a mournful dirge around us.

Hours bled into each other, the fading light painting the sky in shades of bruised purple and angry orange. My muscles ached, and my breath came in ragged gasps, yet I persevered. My human's unwavering faith in me was my fuel. His quiet encouragement and gentle words of praise, when I picked up the trail, were as vital as the oxygen I breathed.

Then, a shift. A change in the wind. A subtle, almost imperceptible difference in the scent. My ears pricked up; my whole body tensed. I had it! The smell was now more pungent, clearer, and more defined. I pulled on the leash excitedly, signaling to my human the change, the shift in the trajectory. He responded instantly; his earlier hesitation was replaced by renewed energy. His grip on the leash tightened not in constraint but in shared purpose. We were a unit again, our anxieties replaced by a focused determination.

The trail led us through a dense thicket, branches snagging at our clothes and undergrowth clinging to our legs. We navigated the obstacles with practiced ease, our movements synchronized and intuitive. He guided me, encouraging me to follow the path the scent revealed, and I, in turn, helped him navigate the dense undergrowth. It was a dance of trust, a symphony of shared purpose.

And then, we saw him—the missing hiker, huddled beneath a rocky overhang, weak but alive. Relief washed over me, a wave of pure, unadulterated joy. My human's reaction was equally profound. He knelt beside the hiker, his relief palpable, his face etched with exhaustion but also the triumph of success.

It was a shared victory, a testament to our enduring bond. But our journey was not solely paved with triumphant rescues. There were setbacks, times when the scent faded, the trail grew cold, and hope seemed to evaporate. Some searches ended in despair, in the bitter taste of failure. One particularly harrowing search stands out in my memory. We searched for days, tirelessly, relentlessly, following every trace, every whisper of a clue. The terrain was brutal and unforgiving, the conditions harsh and demanding. The human element of the search became as challenging as the physical demands of the task.

The weather turned violent, a blizzard descending upon the mountains, blanketing everything in a shroud of blinding white. The search effort, initially focused and determined, began to waver under the relentless onslaught of snow and ice. The exhaustion started to manifest in the humans involved. They were weary, their hope dwindling with each passing hour, and it was also affecting my human. His unwavering confidence, usually my guiding star, was dimming, overshadowed by the crushing weight of the situation. He was becoming increasingly frustrated, visibly shaken by our lack of progress.

I sensed his discouragement; it was not the gruffness of a frustrated trainer but a profound weariness that spoke volumes more than words ever could. I pressed against his hand, seeking comfort and sharing the weight of his burden. We stopped, huddled together for warmth, and he held me, burying his face in my fur. The silence was deafening, broken only by the relentless pounding of the snow and the howling wind. In that shared silence, we found strength; his silent vulnerability, a stark contrast to his usual self-assured demeanor, somehow strengthened our bond. It was a moment of mutual support, a profound unspoken understanding that transcended words.

That night, huddled together against the brutal elements, we were far more than a search and rescue team. We were two souls, bound together by a shared purpose, weathering the storm of doubt and exhaustion. He was a man broken by the weight of the search, and I was the only source of comfort in a vast landscape of ice and snow. As the storm finally subsided and we resumed our search, our shared experience somehow strengthened, making our bond more resilient.

The experience reinforced the knowledge that our triumphs were not solely my achievements; they were reflections of our shared efforts and our unwavering teamwork. Our setbacks, equally, were growth opportunities for strengthening our bond and forging a partnership founded on mutual understanding and steadfast resilience. It wasn't the success of locating a missing person, but also how it highlighted the enduring bond between us in the face of adversity that defined us. The victories and defeats were interwoven, each shaping the other, enriching our partnership, and solidifying our bond. Each shared experience, whether a joyous triumph or a painful setback, added another layer to the rich tapestry of our relationship – a bond forged not in the fire, but in the crucible of shared challenges and triumphs.

CHAPTER 24

Unconditional Love and Loyalty

The scent of woodsmoke and damp earth clung to the air as we returned to the familiar comfort of our home after that harrowing blizzard. He collapsed onto the sofa, his body weary, his spirit subdued. I nudged his hand with my nose, a silent offering of comfort. He sighed a long, drawn-out sound that spoke of equal measures of exhaustion and relief. He scratched behind my ears, his touch gentle, hesitant at first, then growing firmer as if reassuring himself of my presence. That night, I slept curled at his feet, a warm, furry weight against his legs, my presence a silent promise of unwavering support.

Our bond was not simply forged in the fires of intense searching; it was nurtured in the quiet moments and the everyday rituals that defined our life together. He often sat on the porch, watching the sunset, a mug of coffee warming his hands. I would lie at his feet, content to be near him, the rhythmic thump of his heart a comforting presence against the deepening twilight. These quiet moments were as essential as the dramatic rescues.

One rainy afternoon, he was wrestling with a particularly stubborn knot in a piece of rope – a crucial part of his search and rescue equipment. He muttered under his breath, frustration evident in his voice. I watched him struggle, my tail thumping gently against the floor. Finally, he gave a frustrated groan and threw his hands up in the air. At that moment, I saw an opportunity, an instinctive urge to lend a hand. I nudged the rope with my nose, then gently picked it up in my teeth, carefully working the knot loose until it came undone. He looked at me, his eyes wide with surprise and admiration. He chuckled, scratching my head vigorously, a wide grin spread across his face. It was not a dramatic rescue; it was a small act of canine ingenuity, yet the joy and gratitude in his eyes were immense. It was a perfect example of our unspoken communication, our intuitive understanding of one another's needs.

His love went beyond our work together, touching every part of our life. We spent hours playing fetch in the park, his laughter echoing as I chased the ball with boundless energy. He celebrated every success as if it were his own, and it was not the rewards but the pure joy and pride in his eyes that truly mattered.

The bond was not about grand achievements; it was in the small, everyday moments. The gentle scratches behind the ears during a quiet evening at home, the warm, comforting embrace during a storm, the reassuring nudge of my wet nose against his hand during times of uncertainty – these were the threads that wove the rich tapestry of our relationship. In these seemingly mundane interactions, the depth of our connection truly shone through. He would often tell me stories, his voice soft and low, his words flowing like a gentle stream. Even though I could not understand the words, I understood the emotion in his voice and the cadence and rhythm of his speech. It was not about the meaning of the words but about the connection, the sharing of his thoughts and feelings.

One cold winter evening, he came home looking particularly dejected. He had had a difficult day at work, and his usual jovial spirit was absent. He sat quietly on the sofa, his shoulders slumped, his head bowed. I sensed his sadness, his inner turmoil. I crept up to him, nudged his hand with my nose, and rested my head on his lap. He reached down, stroking my fur gently, his touch hesitant at first, then growing firmer, more assured. The simple act of petting me, of sharing the quiet comfort of our mutual presence, seemed to ease his burden. He remained silent for a long time, simply stroking my fur, his deep breaths growing calmer, his shoulders relaxing. I did not need words to understand his sadness; I felt it in the weight of his hand, in the slow, rhythmic strokes of his fingers through my fur. In that shared silence, we found solace, a comfort that transcended words, a testament to the depth of our bond.

His unwavering faith in me was not evident in our professional lives; it permeated every aspect of our relationship. He trusted me implicitly, allowing me to run freely in the park, knowing I would always return to his side. He relied on my intuition, my heightened senses, and my ability to sense danger before it manifested. This trust was not simply given; it was earned through countless shared experiences, marked by unwavering loyalty and dedication on my part. It was a testament to the mutual respect and understanding that formed the foundation of our relationship.

He often spoke of the incredible responsibility of our profession, the weight of lives entrusted to us. But he also spoke of the joy, the immeasurable satisfaction of finding a missing person, reuniting families, and bringing hope back into situations of despair. He emphasized that success was not solely my achievement; it was the result of our collaboration, our teamwork, and our unwavering trust in each other. He understood that our partnership was a two-way street, a dance of mutual respect, where we each contributed our unique skills and abilities. He often said that I was more than a search and rescue dog; I was his partner, confidante, and best friend.

The unconditional love and loyalty that defined our relationship extended beyond our professional lives. It was evident in the quiet moments of companionship, in the shared joys and sorrows, and in the unwavering support we provided each other through challenges. He saw me not simply as a working dog, but as a member of his family —a cherished companion, a true friend. He was not my trainer but my guardian, protector, and best friend. And I, in turn, was his loyal companion, steadfast partner, and unwavering friend. Our bond was not just professional, but deeply personal —a connection that transcended the ordinary. It was a love story written not in words, but in shared experiences, mutual trust, unwavering loyalty —a bond forged in fire and tempered by time. It was a love that words could hardly capture, yet one that permeated every aspect of our lives. It was the kind of love that only a man and his dog could share.

CHAPTER 25
A Partnership for Life

Years blurred into a tapestry woven with threads of shared experiences. The scent of pine needles after a successful search, the comforting weight of his hand on my head during a thunderstorm, the taste of celebratory sausages after a particularly challenging training session – these were the markers of our time together, each a testament to the depth of our connection. He aged, the lines on his face deepening, his hair graying at the temples, yet his eyes still held that spark, that unwavering enthusiasm that had captivated me from the moment we met. Once boundless, my energy began to mellow, my gait slowing, my naps lengthening. But the bond between us remained as strong and vibrant as the day we first met.

One evening, nestled beside him on the porch, he began to reminisce as the last rays of the setting sun painted the sky in orange and purple. He spoke of the early days, my awkward puppyhood, the countless hours spent training, and the moments of doubt and despair, but mostly of triumph. He chuckled, remembering my early attempts at agility, my clumsy tumbles, my almost comical misinterpretations of commands. He described the thrill of our first successful search, the overwhelming relief of finding a lost child, and the joy etched on the faces of their parents. His voice softened as he recounted the challenges, the moments of near misses, the exhaustion that tested our limits, and the emotional toll of dealing with loss. He spoke of the bond forged not through success but through shared adversity.

He spoke of my unwavering loyalty, my ability to sense fear and anxiety in others, and my instinctive understanding of his unspoken commands. He marveled at my sensitivity, my patience, my determination. He confessed that there were times when he questioned his ability to handle the job's pressures, but my unwavering presence and steadfast support had always given him the strength to press on. He often said that I was his anchor, his grounding force, a constant reminder that even in the most chaotic situations, there was always a point of calm, a source of unconditional love. He would pause, gazing out at the distant hills, his expression pensive, lost in his memories. His words painted a vivid picture, not of our shared adventures but of the transformative power of our relationship.

He often recalled a particular search, a desperate hunt for a young girl lost in a dense forest during a violent storm. Rain lashed down, visibility was near zero, and the forest's scent was overwhelming. He was exhausted, hope fading, but I, driven by instinct, pushed through the undergrowth with unwavering determination. He remembered finding her huddled under a fallen tree, shivering but safe. The pure joy and immense relief he felt that day were etched in his memory, a testament to the power of the human-animal bond that transcends language, expectations, and limits.

He spoke about the many lives we touched together, not just the lives we directly saved through our rescue work, but also the lives impacted by witnessing our bond —the unspoken connection between a man and his dog. He described the children who stopped to pet me, their faces alight with wonder, their parents watching with a newfound appreciation for the power of compassion and loyalty. He would point out the quiet moments of connection, the shared silences, the mutual understanding that passed between us without a single word spoken. His voice filled with pride, gratitude, and emotion as he recalled how my unwavering support had become a source of comfort and solace during his most difficult moments.

He confessed that I had taught him patience, resilience, and the importance of unconditional love. He had learned to deeply appreciate the quiet moments, the simple joys of life, the beauty of nature, and the unwavering loyalty of a canine companion. He spoke of the profound impact that I had had on his life, his worldview, and his understanding of the human spirit. He acknowledged that our partnership was not a professional one but a deeply personal and emotional journey that had transformed him in ways he had not anticipated.

As the years continued to unfold, my aging became more pronounced. The once boundless energy that propelled me through countless searches began to fade, replaced by a more gentle, deliberate pace. The youthful exuberance that once defined me mellowed into a quiet confidence, a wisdom born from years of experience and countless shared adventures. Yet, the bond between us remained unshaken. He adapted to my changing needs, and his patience and understanding grew in tandem with my physical limitations.

Our days were now filled with gentler activities: leisurely walks in the park, quiet afternoons spent basking in the sun, and long, contemplative evenings spent together on the porch. He would read to me, his voice a gentle murmur against the backdrop of rustling leaves, and I would rest my head on his lap, content in his presence. Even in silence, our connection remained palpable —a silent conversation woven from shared memories, mutual affection, and a profound understanding that transcended words.

One crisp autumn morning, as the first frosts dusted the ground, I knew it was time. He sat beside me, stroking my fur, tears welling in his eyes. He knew, too. He spoke to me softly, his voice thick with emotion. He thanked me, not for the countless lives I had helped save but for my profound impact on his life. He told me how much I meant to him, how I had filled his life with joy, love, and unwavering companionship. He spoke of our shared adventures, our triumphs, and our struggles, and he thanked me for being the best partner a man could ask for. It was not a farewell but an affirmation of the enduring legacy of our partnership. Our bond, a partnership for life, would remain etched in time, a testament to the profound and transformative nature of the human-animal connection. The love, the loyalty, and the shared experiences were not merely moments, but chapters in a story that would continue to echo through the years to come —a tale of devotion, camaraderie, and love as boundless as the sky above. The legacy of our bond would live on, not in my memory, but in the countless lives we touched, a beacon of hope in a world that often desperately needs it.

CHAPTER 26
The Certification Process

The air crackled with anticipation, a tangible energy vibrating through the ground beneath my paws. The sprawling training grounds, usually a playground of joyous chaos, were now hushed, the usual boisterous energy replaced by a focused intensity. This was not just another training day; it was the culmination of years of relentless work, early morning runs, and countless hours spent honing my skills and mastering commands that once seemed impossible. This was the certification process.

The first challenge was the agility course, a seemingly impossible obstacle course designed to evaluate my physical prowess, obedience, and ability to concentrate under pressure. The course was a symphony of obstacles – a series of A-frames, teeter-totters, tunnels, hurdles, and jumps, each meticulously placed to evaluate my agility, speed, and precision. The scent of freshly cut grass mingled with the heavy nervous tension in the air. My handler, his eyes fixed on me with an unwavering intensity, gave the starting command, his voice a quiet yet powerful force.

I launched into action, my muscles taut, my senses heightened. Each obstacle was conquered with focused precision, a testament to the countless hours we had spent perfecting each move. The A-frames were scaled with effortless grace; the teeter-totters traversed with unwavering balance, and the tunnels navigated with seamless ease. I flew over the hurdles, clearing each one with a mighty leap, my paws barely disturbing the ground. The jumps were cleared with pinpoint accuracy, my landing soft and silent. There was no hesitation, no wavering, only a focused determination to complete the course. Each movement was precise, each transition smooth, a carefully choreographed dance of muscle and instinct, a testament to our unwavering dedication. The finish line was a blur, crossed with a triumphant burst of energy. My handler's hand landed on my head, a gentle caress that spoke volumes more than words ever could.

Next came the obedience trials, a meticulous assessment of my ability to follow commands under pressure in a distracting environment, with a barrage of potentially interfering scents and sounds. The air buzzed with the commands of other dogs, their barks and whimpers, a symphony of canine anxieties. The judges, a panel of experienced trainers and search and rescue professionals, observed with critical eyes, their expressions unreadable. I focused, tuning out the chaos around me, focusing solely on my handler. Each command—sit, stay, down, heel, fetch—was executed precisely, my movements sharp and decisive. I held my position, a statue of canine patience, my gaze unwavering as distractions bombarded my senses. The aroma of other dogs, the cacophony of sounds, the movement around me—all were easily dismissed, my focus unwavering. With each task completed, I received a quiet word of praise from my handler, his approval a silent reassurance.

The final and most crucial test was the area search. The judges had arranged a complex scenario, a simulated missing person situation. I was released into a densely wooded area, the scent of pine needles and damp earth overwhelming. The air throbbed with purpose. My handler remained at a distance, his presence a reassuring anchor.

The scent, faint at first, was elusive, a ghost of a trace. My nose worked tirelessly, analyzing, comparing, eliminating, and pursuing. I moved methodically, covering the ground swiftly, my keen senses constantly at work. The forest floor was a tapestry of scents—decay, earth, vegetation, animals—but I isolated the target, the faint but distinct smell of the 'missing person,' expertly placed by the evaluators.

Each step was deliberate, each turn precise, and every inhalation and exhalation was carefully monitored. The concentration required was profound; my mind was a single-point laser, focused on the task.

I followed the trail, the scent growing stronger with each step. The terrain was challenging—steep inclines, dense undergrowth, fallen logs—but I navigated each obstacle with ease, my instincts guiding me and my powerful body propelling me forward. My heart pounded with the thrill of the chase, yet a quiet confidence filled me.

This was not a game but a real search, a simulated emergency.

Finally, I located the 'missing person,' a dummy carefully placed to simulate the reality of a search. I barked sharply, my voice ringing through the quiet forest, signaling my discovery. My handler rushed to my side; his relief palpable. The judges emerged; their faces etched with professional approval. The evaluation was thorough, examining not only my ability to locate the target but also my overall performance, including my stamina, obedience, and focus.

The certification was not a test of my skills but a culmination of our shared journey. The years of training, countless hours spent honing my abilities, and the unwavering bond forged between us all culminated in this moment. The intensity, the pressure, the focus – everything had been worth it. It was a test not of my abilities, but of our team —a testament to the partnership we had built, a relationship founded on mutual trust and respect.

After what seemed like an eternity but was probably only a few minutes, the head judge approached us. His few words, though, carried the weight of years of experience and countless evaluations. He announced, clear and precise, that I had passed the test. The certification was official.

The relief was immense, and a wave of emotion washed over us both. Years of dedication, countless hours of training, unwavering commitment, and shared sacrifices – all were validated in this moment. The weight of responsibility settled upon my shoulders, a responsibility I embraced with pride and unwavering commitment. I was no longer a dog; I was a certified search and rescue dog, a guardian, a lifesaver. The journey had been long and challenging, filled with moments of doubt and triumph, sweat and tears, as well as failures and successes. But it had ultimately led us to this: the fulfillment of our shared dream.

My handler hugged me tightly. The silent exchange was profound, a wordless conversation that encompassed everything we had been through. His eyes, usually brimming with playful affection, were now shining with pride, reflecting my accomplishment. It was not my certification; it was a symbol of our partnership, our collaboration, and our enduring bond.

The certification was not a badge of honor, but a symbol of our commitment, our shared purpose, a testament to years of hard work and dedication, and a symbol of our unwavering belief in one another. It was a promise to help those in need, a promise to be there for those who are lost and vulnerable, a promise to bring hope and solace in times of despair. It was a testament to our combined strength, resilience, ability to overcome challenges, unwavering determination, deep mutual respect, and unbreakable bond.

We were ready. We were a team, certified and prepared to face whatever challenges lay ahead. Our lives, intertwined and deeply interconnected, were now dedicated to a higher purpose —one that would evaluate us, challenge us, and also reward us in ways we could not even imagine.

CHAPTER 27

Demonstrating Skills and Abilities

The final evaluation loomed; a crucible forged in the fires of rigorous training. The air hung heavy with the scent of anticipation, a mixture of pine needles and damp earth, punctuated by the faint, almost imperceptible, aroma of the simulated missing person. My handler, a figure of unwavering calm amidst the swirling anxieties of the other teams, gave me a reassuring pat on the head. His touch was a grounding force, a silent reassurance that resonated deep within my core.

The scenario was complex, a meticulously crafted puzzle designed to push me to my limits. We were in a vast, sprawling field, a landscape of rolling hills and dense patches of woodland. The judges, seasoned professionals with decades of experience between them, watched from a distance, their expressions inscrutable. Their silence was more intense than any shouted command, an unspoken challenge to prove my worth.

The command came, a simple release, and I was off. My powerful legs propelled me forward, my senses hyper-alert, as I dissected the myriad scents that assaulted my nostrils. The wind carried the whispers of a thousand different fragrances – decaying leaves, fresh earth, the lingering scent of wild animals, and the metallic tang of distant machinery. But my mind was a sieve, filtering out the irrelevant, focusing solely on the faintest trace of the target scent. It was a subtle difference, a ghost in the symphony of smells, but I could detect it, a tiny thread of hope in the immensity of the natural world.

The search was a testament to my training, which culminated in years of dedicated work. Every muscle, every sinew, every instinct was honed to perfection, a symphony of precision and efficiency. I moved with a quiet purpose, my movements precise and economical, covering the ground swiftly but systematically. My nose was a compass guiding me across the uneven terrain. I weaved through patches of thorny bushes, leaped over fallen logs, and navigated treacherous inclines with a grace that belied the difficulty of the task. My handler remained a silent observer, his presence a reassuring anchor in the vastness of the search area.

The scent, initially elusive, grew steadily stronger. I followed it, relentlessly pursuing the trail, my heart pounding with excitement and determination. Each step was calculated, and each inhalation was a purposeful intake of information. My whole being was focused on this singular goal, and nothing else existed. The world around me seemed to fade, replaced by an intense, all-consuming focus on the task.

The terrain grew tougher, with thicker undergrowth and a more complex scent, yet I persevered, guided by instinct and unwavering determination. I pushed through brambles that snagged my fur, navigated slippery rocks, and even lost the scent briefly before picking it up again. Each obstacle strengthened my resolve. The judges were impressed by my tenacity, speed, and ability to stay focused despite the challenging environment.

The moment of discovery was electric. The scent intensified, becoming sharp and unmistakable. I located the "missing person," a dummy carefully positioned by the judges to evaluate my accuracy. A sharp bark pierced the silence of the woods, a triumphant howl that echoed through the trees. I stood over the dummy, my tail wagging, my body radiating a palpable sense of achievement.

The judges emerged, their faces betraying a mixture of astonishment and admiration. They observed my performance, examining every detail – the precision of my search pattern, the efficiency of my movements, and my response to the find. Their evaluation was thorough, but their approval was evident. They examined my responses, noting my stamina, ability to maintain focus, and obedience to commands, even in the face of distractions.

Their praise was silent, delivered in nods and appreciative glances, but it spoke volumes more than any words could have. Their silence confirmed that they had witnessed something special, not the accomplishment of a highly trained search and rescue dog, but the testament to years of dedication and the unwavering bond between

handler and dog. I had demonstrated not just skill and ability, but also heart and steadfast loyalty.

The certification ceremony was brief, a simple formality after the intense trial. Yet, the weight of the moment was immense. The official announcement, the handing over of the certificate, the solemn handshake between my handler and the head judge—it was the culmination of years of relentless effort, sweat and tears, early mornings, and late nights. It was a shared accomplishment, a partnership ratified by an official recognition of excellence. I passed. I was certified.

The journey to this point had been challenging, filled with moments of doubt, frustration, and even fear. But those challenges only made me stronger, more resilient, and more focused. They had forged a bond between my handler and myself that was unbreakable. The certification was more than a badge; it symbolized our unwavering commitment to one another, a testament to the power of teamwork and the magic of the human-animal bond. We were ready. We were a team, forged in the fires of relentless training, bound together by unwavering loyalty and mutual respect, and prepared to face whatever challenges lay ahead. Our adventure, our shared purpose, was only beginning.

CHAPTER 28
The Moment of Truth

The crisp autumn air nipped at my ears as I stood beside my handler, the scent of damp earth and pine needles sharp in my nostrils. The certification ceremony was not a grand affair, with no fanfare or cheering crowds. It was a simple affair, held in a small, unassuming building adjacent to the vast training grounds —a place that had witnessed countless hours of sweat, tears, and unwavering dedication. Yet, the atmosphere was thick with anticipation, a palpable tension hanging in the air, shared not just by my handler and me but also by all the other canine candidates and their handlers who had reached this pivotal moment.

We had endured the grueling training, pushing ourselves and our canine partners to the limits of strength and skill. Some challenges were minor, others seemed insurmountable, yet here we stood, on the brink of success.

The head judge, a woman whose eyes held the wisdom of decades spent working alongside dogs, approached us. Her demeanor was serious, yet there was a glint of something else in her gaze –admiration, perhaps? Or maybe something akin to pride? She spoke a few words, but her tone was filled with a quiet respect that resonated deeply within me. She held the certificate, a crisp, official document —a tangible representation of all they had achieved together. The paper felt stiff and cool against my handler's fingertips as he accepted it, a silent acknowledgment of the immense effort behind that seemingly simple piece of paper.

My handler's hand rested lightly on my head, a comforting presence that eased the slight tremor of anticipation that thrummed through me. His touch conveyed more than mere affection; it was a reassurance, a silent communication that transcended words. It was the understanding look between two partners who had shared an extraordinary journey, facing challenges together, celebrating victories together, and forging an unshakeable bond in the process. At that moment, the rigorous training sessions, the early morning runs, the grueling obstacle courses – all of it seemed to fade into the background, leaving only the profound sense of accomplishment and shared triumph. This certificate was not about passing a test; it was a testament to our unwavering commitment to each other and our shared dreams and aspirations.

The quiet solemnity of the moment was broken only by the soft rustle of the certificate, the gentle clinking of metal as the head judge fastened a small, engraved tag to my collar – a mark of distinction, a symbol of my official status as a certified search and rescue dog. The weight of it, both literally and metaphorically, was considerable. It was a badge of honor earned through relentless effort, perseverance, and an unwavering belief in the power of our partnership. But it was also a weight of responsibility, a reminder of the crucial role we would play in the lives of others.

After the formal ceremony, a wave of relief washed over me, a feeling so profound and overwhelming that it was almost physical.

The tension that coiled within me throughout the training period finally dissipated, leaving behind an exhilarating lightness. The muscles in my body, previously taut with anticipation, relaxed. My tail thumped against the ground with a joyous rhythm, a physical manifestation of the happiness that surged through me. I had passed. I was certified. And even more importantly, I had done so alongside my best friend, my handler.

The joy was not confined to me; I could also sense it radiating from my handler. His smile was wide and genuine, reflecting the pride he felt in our shared accomplishment. He knelt beside me, his fingers gently stroking my fur, whispering words of encouragement and praise. The words were vague but filled with emotion. It was a moment of profound connection, a silent conversation between two beings who understood each other implicitly, a bond forged through shared experience and unwavering loyalty.

The celebrations that followed were understated but deeply meaningful. There were no extravagant parties or public accolades; instead, a quiet gathering of fellow handlers and their canine partners took place, a celebration held in the heart of the training grounds —a place that had witnessed our struggles and triumphs. We shared stories, swapped experiences, and reminisced about our journey together. Each handler had a tale of their own, filled with joy and frustration, success, and near-failure moments. It was a camaraderie forged in the fires of shared challenges, a bond that only those who had undergone the arduous process of training a search and rescue dog could fully understand.

As I reflected on the journey that had brought me to this moment, memories flooded back – the early days of puppyhood, the playful nips and exuberant tumbles, the first tentative steps in obedience training, the frustration of missed commands and the joy of finally mastering a new skill; the thrill of the agility course, the exhilaration of learning a challenging obstacle; the intensity of the scent detection exercises, the focused concentration required to discern the faintest trace of a scent amidst a cacophony of aromas; and finally, the emotional weight of the search exercises, the responsibility of finding a missing person. Every memory, both happy and challenging, has played a crucial role in shaping me into the person I am today, capable not only of performing the technical aspects of the job but also of possessing the empathy and understanding needed to support and comfort those who genuinely need assistance.

My handler and I had spent countless hours perfecting our teamwork, refining our communication, and forging an unbreakable bond of trust. This bond, more than any technical skill, had made the difference. It had been the unseen thread connecting all the individual elements of our training, transforming a series of disparate exercises into a unified, cohesive whole. It was the foundation upon which our success had been built. Mutual respect, unwavering loyalty, and shared purpose were the authentic ingredients of our triumph. And this understanding extended beyond the individual training sessions.

The night after our certification, we sat together as the moon glowed gently upon the training grounds. The air held a quiet stillness, the sounds of nature replacing the previous din of activity. In that moment of tranquility, I truly grasped the weight of my new role. The certification was not an official recognition of my abilities but a solemn vow to dedicate my life to serving others. The joy of the certification was only half of the equation. The understanding of the immense responsibility I now bore was the other.

As I lay my head on my handler's lap, the warmth of his hand gently stroking my fur, I knew we were ready. The arduous training had been merely a preparation, a prelude to the true adventure ahead. Our journey had only begun. We were prepared to face whatever challenges the future might hold, confident in our abilities, unshakeable in our bond, and committed to the sacred task of helping those in need. The shared experience of the training program fostered a bond that extended far beyond the practical aspects of search and rescue. It was a kinship born from mutual respect, a partnership forged in the fires of relentless training, and a foundation of unwavering loyalty upon which future successes would be built and the moment of certification marked not a culmination of our hard work but the initiation of a lifelong mission—a shared endeavor of dedication, service, and the extraordinary connection between a human and their canine companion. In that connection, I discovered my purpose and a profound sense of belonging. The world stretched before us, filled with possibilities, and we, a unified team, were ready to meet them.

CHAPTER 29
Embracing the Challenge

The crisp morning air, usually invigorating, now held a different quality-a tautness, a breathless anticipation that mirrored my own. My handler, usually a picture of calm efficiency, paced restlessly, his movements betraying the nervous energy thrumming beneath the surface. Today was the day—our first official search and rescue mission.

The training had prepared us, drilling into the procedures, techniques, and the importance of unwavering focus and obedience. We had mastered the agility courses, the scent detection exercises, and the area searches, each step a building block in the edifice of our preparedness. But theory and practice were different beasts. The controlled environment of the training grounds, with its familiar scents and predictable challenges, paled in comparison to the unpredictable reality of a real-world search.

The briefing was short, sharp, and efficient. The missing person, an elderly woman with dementia, had wandered from her assisted living facility hours earlier. The last sighting placed her near a densely wooded area, a maze of tangled undergrowth and unpredictable terrain. The description stirred a primal instinct in me, sharpening my senses and heightening my awareness of every detail around me.

My handler's hand rested on my head, a reassuring pressure calming my excitement. His eyes, usually sparkling with laughter, held a seriousness that matched the gravity of the situation. He spoke a few words, primarily instructions, a low, steady murmur that cut through the apprehensive silence of the gathering team. The other search and rescue teams, their dogs equally poised and attentive, stood ready, their collective energy a tangible force. This was no game; this was a race against time, a desperate search for a vulnerable human life.

We were part of a larger team, a coordinated unit of humans and canines, each with a specific role. My handler's expertise was strategically guiding our search pattern, utilizing my superior olfactory abilities to navigate the complex terrain and notice the faintest trace of the missing woman's scent. The other teams covered a wider area using different strategies, a combined approach that optimized the chances of finding her quickly. Effective communication between teams would be crucial, and I knew I had to remain responsive and attentive to my handler's every command.

The woods were a different world. The sun struggled to penetrate the dense canopy, casting long, eerie shadows that danced and writhed in my peripheral vision. The familiar scents of pine and damp earth were now overlaid with a complex tapestry of other aromas—decaying leaves, animal droppings, and the subtle scent of human presence. My handler's guidance, through hand signals and low whispers, steered me through this olfactory maze. My focus was absolute, every sense honed to its peak acuity.

Each step was deliberate, each inhalation a concentrated effort to decipher the countless scents bombarding my nostrils. The task was not simply to detect the smell of a human; it was to discern the specific scent of the missing woman amidst the myriad of other scents, a process that demanded immense patience and unwavering focus. The intensity of the work smell was physically and mentally demanding, requiring a concentration that pushed me to my limits.

My handler's whispered encouragement kept me going, his presence a reassuring anchor in the confusing chaos of the woods. He spoke in short bursts, his tone never raised, never insistent; instead, he communicated through subtle shifts in body language, a nuanced dance of communication between handler and canine. Occasionally, he would offer me brief moments of rest, allowing me to recover from the intense concentration. But these were brief interludes, and soon, I was back at the task at hand, my senses laser-focused on the mission.

The hours stretched on, the silence of the woods broken only by the rustling of leaves and the occasional bird call. Doubts began to creep in, a chilling whisper that threatened to undermine my unwavering focus. But the determination in my handler's eyes, the steadfast belief in our abilities, pushed back against the encroaching despair. We pressed on, unyielding in our pursuit, undeterred by the obstacles.

Then, it happened. A subtle shift in the air, a faint but unmistakable change in the olfactory landscape. A new scent layered over the familiar aromas of the woods – the smell of the missing woman, faint but persistent. My tail thumped softly against the undergrowth as I locked onto the scent, my body straining forward, every muscle alert and ready for action.

The pursuit was intense, a silent chase guided by the faintest threads of a scent. We navigated fallen logs, climbed over undergrowth, and weaved our way through dense vegetation, a harmonious team moving with precision. The terrain was demanding, but my stamina, built through rigorous training, held firm. I followed the scent, the intensity increasing with each step. The exhilaration of the chase was intense, an emotional high that fueled my efforts, an adrenaline rush that sharpened my senses.

Then, I saw her. She was huddled beneath a large oak tree, frail yet alive, her eyes wide with a mix of relief and fear. My handler rushed forward, his joy unrestrained as he gently approached and comforted her. The other search and rescue teams arrived moments later, relief etched on their faces. The successful culmination of the mission was an overwhelming surge of happiness and satisfaction. We had found her, and at that moment, I understood the true meaning of our work.

The journey back was a quiet procession; the woods were no longer dark and menacing, but filled with accomplishment and profound gratitude. My handler's hand rested on my head, a gentle stroke of affection. I knew then that the certification had been the beginning, a mere threshold to a life of service filled with challenges and untold rewards. The quiet solemnity of the moment transcended words, a testament to our shared experience, a powerful bond forged in the fires of determination and success. The feeling was indescribable, a mixture of pride, relief, and an overwhelming sense of purpose.

The experience left an indelible mark on me, an understanding that went beyond the technical skills I had mastered. It was the recognition of the profound impact we could have, the realization that our work was more than a job; it was a calling, a sacred duty. This first official mission marked not only the beginning of my career as a search and rescue dog but also the initiation of a lifelong commitment to serving others. This devotion would shape and define my life. It was a testament to the bond between my handler and me, a partnership forged in rigorous training and solidified in the heart of the woods. The world felt different now, filled with a newfound sense of purpose and the promise of countless other adventures, each bringing new challenges and new opportunities to serve. The bond with my handler was stronger than ever, a partnership founded on mutual respect, shared commitment, and the unbreakable connection between a human and their dog.

CHAPTER 30
Preparation and Training Continue

The certification ceremony felt like a mere punctuation mark, a complete stop at the end of one sentence, immediately followed by an ellipsis, hinting at the vast, unwritten chapters ahead. The celebratory atmosphere, the proud smiles of my handler and the other handlers, and the warm congratulations faded quickly into the background as the reality of ongoing commitment settled in. Certification was not the finish line; it was merely the starting gate.

The following weeks were a whirlwind of continued training and a relentless pursuit of excellence that exceeded the minimum requirements for certification. We did not maintain our skills; we sharpened and honed them to a razor's edge. Once a source of playful competition, agility courses evolved into rigorous exercises in precision and speed, with each run analyzed and every movement scrutinized. Scent detection exercises were no longer straightforward games of hide-and-seek; they transformed into complex scenarios designed to challenge and refine my ability to isolate specific scents amidst a cacophony of olfactory distractions. We practiced in diverse environments, ranging from bustling city streets to the quiet serenity of open fields, where each location presented a unique set of challenges and opportunities for adaptation and improvement. My handler, a man of unwavering dedication, pushed me beyond my perceived limits, demanding unwavering focus and obedience.

He was not training me; he was molding me, refining my raw talent into a finely tuned search and rescue instrument. He introduced new techniques, advanced strategies, and ever-evolving methods to enhance our efficiency and effectiveness in the field. He understood that true mastery was not about achieving a certain level of proficiency, but rather a continuous striving for improvement —a relentless pursuit of perfection. Our training was not confined to physical exercises; it also extended to mental acuity. We worked on developing a deeper understanding of each other, achieving a seamless synergy that transcended verbal communication. His subtle shifts in body language became my guiding stars, his whispers transforming into clear, concise instructions. We built a fine-tuned communication system in which we anticipated each other's movements and reactions with an intuitive understanding. This silent, unspoken conversation was a testament to our bond, a partnership forged in trust and mutual respect.

However, the training was not solely focused on me. My handler, too, was constantly undergoing his professional development. He attended advanced training workshops, participated in seminars, and remained updated on the latest search and rescue techniques and technologies. He kept meticulous records of our training sessions, analyzing our progress and adjusting his methods accordingly. He understood that being a successful search and rescue handler was about his competence and providing me with the best possible training and care.

He frequently attended conferences and workshops, where he networked with other handlers, exchanged ideas, and shared experiences. He was always eager to learn, continually seeking ways to enhance his skills and stay ahead of the curve. He considered it his duty not only to refine my abilities but also to elevate the standards of search and rescue practice. His relentless pursuit of knowledge and improvement was as important as any training exercise we undertook.

The ongoing education extended beyond the technical aspects of the job. We practiced working within a larger team and understanding the importance of communication and coordination. We participated in simulated search and rescue scenarios, rehearsing the various procedures and protocols crucial in real-life situations. These simulations were not mere exercises but invaluable opportunities to develop our ability to work under pressure, maintain focus amidst chaos, and adapt to unexpected challenges. They were also crucial in understanding the psychology of emergency response, developing empathy for those in distress, and managing expectations during high-pressure missions.

One particularly challenging exercise involved a simulated night search in a densely wooded area, with obstacles strategically placed to evaluate our skills and stamina. The darkness and unfamiliar terrain intensified the exercise, demanding every ounce of our focus and cooperation. The darkness was a new layer of complexity, adding the challenge of navigating through the woods in near-complete darkness, relying solely on my sense of smell and my handler's skillful guidance. This test highlighted the importance of trust and communication, pushing our partnership to its limits and further cementing the bond.

Another exercise focused on working amidst distractions. We practiced searching in areas with significant background noise –simulated construction sounds, traffic, and crowds. The challenge was to filter out irrelevant scents and focus on the specific target amidst many competing odors. The ability to filter out distractions is crucial in real-life scenarios, which can often be unpredictable and chaotic.

The rigorous training schedule was not always easy to follow. There were days when I was tired, frustrated, and ready to give up. Sometimes, my handler's demands seemed excessive, pushing me beyond my capabilities. However, through perseverance, patience, and unwavering mutual respect, we always managed to push through. The rewards far outweighed the challenges, and the satisfaction of mastering a new skill or completing a challenging exercise was a powerful motivator.

Our training was not just physical and mental; it also demanded emotional resilience. We had to manage the intense stress of searching for missing persons, face the possibility of finding someone deceased, and shoulder the immense responsibility of each mission. My handler's role extended beyond guiding my physical actions; he was my mentor, confidante, and emotional support system. He understood the psychological demands of our profession and guided me through the emotional rollercoaster, ensuring that our work did not damage us in the long run.

The ongoing commitment to training and development was not merely a professional requirement, but a testament to our dedication —a reflection of our shared commitment to excellence. It was not about finding missing people but about constantly striving for excellence and being prepared for whatever challenges the future might bring. Pursuing knowledge and expertise was an ongoing process, never complete, continually evolving, and constantly adapting. It was an integral part of our journey, a constant companion in our quest to make a tangible difference in the world. And in that ceaseless pursuit, we found a deeper and more fulfilling bond —a testament to the extraordinary relationship between a human and their canine partner, a connection built not on love and loyalty, but on shared purpose and relentless dedication to a greater cause.

CHAPTER 31
A Mountain Rescue

The crisp mountain air bit at my nose, starkly contrasting the familiar scents of the training grounds. The familiar smell of pine and damp earth was laced with a new, sharp tang – the metallic bite of fear. My handler, his face etched with a grim determination, adjusted my harness. The usual pre-mission banter was absent, replaced by a tense silence that spoke volumes. This was not a simulated exercise; this was real. A young hiker, separated from his group during a sudden blizzard, was missing on the treacherous slopes of Mount Baldy. The swirling snow reduced visibility to near zero, and the temperature plummeted rapidly.

The helicopter ride was a blur of whirling wind and whiteout conditions. My handler held me close, his presence a comforting anchor in the swirling chaos. As we descended, the wind buffeted the helicopter, the rhythmic thump of the rotors a constant drum against my ears. Below, the mountain loomed, a jagged, unforgiving landscape shrouded in snow. The moment our feet touched the ground, the reality of the situation hit me with full force. The wind howled relentlessly, tearing at my fur, the snow stinging my eyes. The biting cold penetrated my thick coat, a chilling reminder of the situation's urgency. My handler quickly briefed me, his voice barely audible above the wind's roar. He pointed towards a faint trail, almost swallowed by the deepening snow. This was where the hiker was last seen.

My nose went to work, sifting through the complex tapestry of scents that battled against the relentless wind. The air was thick with the smell of pine, damp earth, and the faint, fleeting aroma of a human—the lost hiker. But it was faint, almost lost within the overwhelming scents of the mountain. The snow, while obscuring the trail, strangely preserved the hiker's scent. The scent was weak and fragmented, but it was there.

We moved slowly, deliberately, following the trail, my handler guiding me through deep snow and treacherous ice patches. The mountain was a labyrinth of snow-covered trees, its slopes hidden beneath a blanket of blinding white. Each step was a challenge, demanding both strength and precision. My paws sank deep into the snow with every step, the effort slowing our pace. My handler adjusted his pace to my movements, the silent choreography of our teamwork. He understood that pushing me too hard would only hinder our efforts.

As we proceeded, the snow grew deeper. My handler moved strategically, evaluating the snow's stability at every turn, using his snowshoes to stabilize particularly precarious spots. At times, I felt the snow threatening to engulf us. Yet, my determination, fueled by the hope of finding the missing hiker, kept me pushing forward. Hours passed, the wind still screaming, the snow relentlessly falling. My handler's body language shifts became increasingly vital. His minimal gestures, the almost imperceptible changes in his posture, were my compass, guiding me through the blizzard. The faint scent led us through a dense stand of pines, their branches heavy with snow.

And then, I caught it—a more potent, sharper scent. It was unmistakable, a distinct human scent, stronger and closer than anything I had detected. It was the scent of fear, mingled with the smell of woodsmoke and damp wool. I pulled at my leash, excitedly alerting my handler. He noticed the subtle change in my behavior, the shift in my posture, and my increased attention to the ground. He followed my lead, his eyes scanning the terrain with a growing intensity.

We emerged from the pine trees, and the hiker was huddled beneath a massive, snow-laden rock. He was shivering uncontrollably, his face pale with exhaustion and cold, but he was alive. Relief washed over me, a wave of profound satisfaction that swept away the exhaustion of the arduous search. Though weak from exposure, he was unharmed. My handler radioed for assistance, and we stayed with him, offering warmth and reassurance until help arrived. As the helicopter appeared through the snowy sky, a deep sense of accomplishment and purpose filled me like never before.

The descent back was far easier; the weight on my heart was lifted. I snuggled against my handler, the warmth of his body a comforting contrast to the frigid air. The helicopter ride was quieter this time, a peaceful journey punctuated by the happy chirps of my handler over the comms. Only when the ground came closer, the snow-covered landscape blurring into smaller patterns of white and brown, did I begin to feel the effects of exhaustion.

Back at the base, the cheers and handshakes were a welcome reward, but the real reward was the quiet understanding I shared with my handler, a knowing smile, a gentle pat on the head – the silent language of a partnership forged in the face of adversity. The warmth and gratitude that filled the air made it clear how necessary the successful rescue was. The families were worried, the search party was tired, and the hiker was safe. It was not about the accolades or the recognition, but the quiet satisfaction that came with a job well done, a life saved. The mountain wind may have whipped, the snow may have fallen, and the cold may have threatened to claim our lives, but in the end, the bond between us, handler and dog, had prevailed.

The next few days, with media attention, interviews, and celebratory dinners, were a blur. However, the images of the blizzard, the treacherous slopes, and the lost hiker's relief remained etched in my memory, a testament to the gravity of our work and a reminder of our profound responsibility. The experience strengthened our bond, refining our teamwork to an almost telepathic level. The quiet exchanges, subtle cues, and shared understanding were the hallmarks of our evolving partnership. Whether successful or challenging, each mission contributed to our growth, shaping us into a cohesive unit —a single entity driven by a shared purpose.

Each new mission presented a different set of challenges, refining our skills in countless ways, from the bustling city streets, where a thousand other odors masked the scent of a lost child, to the dense, unforgiving forests, where every footfall tested the limits of our resilience and abilities. Every search was a lesson, a chance to improve, adapt, and refine the quiet, efficient partnership between man and dog. The shared moments of success and the painful acknowledgment of situations that did not end in happy reunions were all part of the narrative that strengthened our professional and personal bond. There were losses and times when we searched tirelessly, only to find the worst possible outcome.

These experiences tested the limits of my resilience and forced us to grapple with the realities of search and rescue. But even in failure, there was growth, learning, and a shared understanding that transcended words, reinforcing the unbreakable bond between handler and dog.

The rigorous training continued, each practice session sharpening our skills, building our endurance, and reinforcing the trust that was the bedrock of our partnership. We practiced scent detection in increasingly complex settings, simulating real-world scenarios that tested my ability to focus amid distractions. We practiced in extreme conditions—blizzards, torrential rains, and sweltering heat—to prepare ourselves for any eventuality. Each training exercise honed my abilities, strengthened my senses, enhanced my stamina, and refined cooperation between handler and dog. Our training was not only about physical prowess but about mental agility and emotional resilience, the ability to handle the stress, and the emotional turmoil that came with facing the reality of missing persons. The journey to becoming a search and rescue team was a continuous evolution, a relentless pursuit of mastery, and a shared journey that transformed us both.

CHAPTER 32

A Search in the City

The city was a cacophony of sounds and smells, starkly contrasting the silent, snow-covered mountains. The crisp mountain air was replaced by a thick, humid blanket, heavy with exhaust fumes, hot asphalt, and a thousand other urban aromas. This was a different kind of search, a different type of challenge. Instead of the stark simplicity of snow and pine, we faced the overwhelming complexity of a sprawling metropolis, a labyrinth of concrete and steel, a bewildering maze of scents and sounds.

My handler, whose usual calm demeanor had been replaced by a focused intensity, adjusted my harness. He briefed me, his voice low and steady, a reassuring counterpoint to the urban din. A young girl named Lily had wandered away from her grandmother during a crowded street festival. Hours had passed, and the police, despite their best efforts, had yet to find her. The urgency was palpable, the pressure immense, but unlike the mountain search, this felt...different. There was a different kind of energy here, a frenetic pulse that thrummed beneath the surface of the city's chaotic rhythm.

The search began at the heart of the festival, a swirling vortex of people, music, and the tantalizing aroma of street food. The sheer volume of competing scents was initially overwhelming, a sensory overload that threatened to drown out Lily's trace. With its relative simplicity, the mountain was a far cry from the chaotic olfactory landscape of a city teeming with millions of humans, animals, vehicles, and a lifetime of various scents embedded in the concrete itself. The task here was not about following a scent trail; it was about filtering through a blizzard of olfactory information, isolating Lily's scent from the overwhelming symphony of urban smells.

My handler, a master of subtle cues, guided me through the throngs of people, his hand steady on my lead. His movements were almost imperceptible, a silent dance that allowed us to navigate the crowded streets without disturbing the flow of the festival. He knew I needed the space to work, concentrate, and sift through the myriad scents bombarding my nose. This was a different kind of partnership, a more intricate and demanding ballet than the straightforward tracking we had performed on the mountain.

I worked methodically, my nose to the ground, my senses hyper-alert. Each inhalation was a journey, carefully analyzing the complex blend of smells. The scent of popcorn, hot dogs, and cotton candy mingled with the perfume of flowers, the sweat of the crowds, and the exhaust fumes from passing cars. It was a sensory overload, but I persisted, my focus unwavering, my determination fueled by the hope of finding Lily.

The first few hours were frustrating. Lily's scent was faint, fragmented, almost lost within the swirling mass of other odors. Unlike the snow's ability to preserve scent in the mountains, the city's concrete and asphalt seemed to absorb and diffuse smells, making my task considerably harder. The scent would appear, a tantalizing flicker, then vanish again, swallowed by the city's cacophony of aromas. Doubt began to creep in, a subtle tremor of uncertainty, and this time, it was not the cold or the wind but the sheer density and dynamism of the city's environment.

But then, my handler's keen eye noticed something crucial, initially a faint hint, an almost imperceptible sign: a discarded candy wrapper. It was small and insignificant, easily overlooked, yet to me, it was a beacon, a breadcrumb in the city's vast and complex landscape. The scent, faint as it was, clung to the wrapper, a tenacious reminder of Lily's presence.

From there, the trail grew clearer, though the challenge remained. I followed it through crowded streets, weaving between people and sidestepping obstacles with practiced ease. My handler guided me with precise, almost silent commands, our understanding near telepathic. The city's cacophony continued, yet its rhythm seemed to shift, sharpening my focus and making the goal crystal clear.

The scent led us to a quiet alleyway hidden behind a bustling marketplace. The air here was thick with the smell of garbage, damp concrete, and Lily's familiar scent. It was stronger now, more distinct, and infused with a hint of fear, a subtle note that tightened my gut. I pulled at my leash, alerting my handler, and my bark was a mixture of excitement and concern. He found her huddled in a corner, shivering and scared but unharmed. Relief washed over me; a wave of emotion so intense it almost knocked me off my feet. It was the same feeling as when we found the hiker on the mountain, only this time surrounded by the roar of a city, its sounds, and smells now a source of joyous relief.

Lily's grandmother rushed to her, embracing her tightly. The scene was a heart-wrenching tableau of relief and reunion, a stark reminder of the importance of our work. It was a powerful counterpoint to the vast urban environment around us and the quiet intensity of our search. When I returned to the police station, I was met with cheers and congratulations, but I barely registered them. My mind was still processing the contrast between the mountain search and this one. The mountain had been a test of endurance, a battle against the elements. On the other hand, the city had been a test of my concentration, a challenge to my ability to filter and decipher scents within an overwhelming sensory environment. It was a different world, with a different set of skills and strategies, but the result was the same in both places – a successful rescue and the quiet satisfaction that comes with a job well done. The contrast between the two highlighted how adaptable we would both become.

Curled at my handler's feet that night, I reviewed the day's events. The two searches, so different in their settings and challenges, had both underscored the importance of our partnership, the quiet understanding between handler and dog, and the seamless teamwork that allowed us to navigate different landscapes and overcome distinct obstacles. With its relentless cacophony, the city was far from the quiet solitude of the mountains, but it presented its special rewards.

The triumphant return of Lily and the reunion with her family were far different in tone than the quiet relief of a mountain rescue, but both were equally satisfying. We have saved lives, located missing persons, and fulfilled our duties effectively. The work of a search and rescue team does not exist in a vacuum; each mission is a part of a larger whole, a series of experiences that shape and refine our skills and relationships.

CHAPTER 33
Working in Extreme Conditions

The biting wind howled like a banshee, tearing at my fur and stinging my eyes with icy pellets. Already several feet deep, the snow continued to fall, a relentless blizzard that transformed the familiar mountain landscape into a blinding white void. This was no ordinary search; this was a fight for survival, a test of endurance that pushed my handler and me to our absolute limits. The thin and frigid air burned in my lungs with each labored breath. Despite their thick padding, my paws were beginning to ache as the relentless cold seeped into my bones.

This mission was different. We were not tracking the familiar scent of lost hikers but a faint, almost imperceptible trace of a young boy named Ethan, who had wandered away from his family during a winter camping trip. Hours had passed, and the temperature had plummeted, increasing the urgency tenfold. Each passing minute diminished Ethan's chances of survival. The cold was our enemy, and time was quickly running out.

My handler, his face partially obscured by a balaclava, moved with a cautious determination, his every step measured and deliberate. He was bundled in layers of thermal gear, but even this minimal protection against the bitter elements was insufficient. The conditions were perilous; hypothermia was a real threat for both of us. He checked on me frequently, ensuring my body temperature remained safe and supplementing my water supply with a specially formulated, warm broth to combat extreme conditions.

The snow was relentless. Each gust of wind deposited a fresh layer of powder over our tracks, making the search even harder. The wind and snow constantly erased the familiar scent trail we relied on, turning the search into a seemingly endless task. My nose, usually so dependable, struggled in the whiteout. The blizzard was more than a weather phenomenon; it was a physical and mental barrier, a force of nature that threatened to overwhelm us at every turn. The constant and forceful wind played havoc with my sense of smell, carrying scents in unpredictable patterns. It was like solving a complex puzzle with missing pieces and ever-changing parameters.

My handler understood my struggle. He used visual cues with the scent: how the snow had been disturbed and the slight break in the snow pattern. Even the way the wind bent the branches became an important clue. He was an exceptional handler who learned to listen to me in a way that many others would not, learning how to interpret not just the barks and whines but also the subtleties of my posture and movements. We continued for what felt like an eternity, our bodies numb with cold, our spirits tested by the unforgiving conditions. Doubt gnawed at the edges of my concentration, a chilling whisper in the back of my mind. Yet, I pushed through the pain, the discomfort, and the doubt, fueled by the unwavering belief that Ethan was out there, somewhere in this white expanse of snow, still alive and waiting.

Then, a faint shift in the wind, a subtle change in the direction of the scent. It was almost imperceptible, but my sensitive nose detected it, a hint of something different in the frigid air – a slightly warmer scent, a trace of Ethan's body heat amidst the overwhelming coldness of the air. I pulled on my leash, my barks echoing through the blizzard, a signal to my handler that we were close. He followed my lead, his movements careful and precise. Soon, I found him—partially buried beneath a snowdrift, shivering uncontrollably, but miraculously, still alive. Relief washed over me, a wave of pure emotion, as the grim and cold landscape suddenly burst with vibrant, life-giving energy.

Even after finding him, the rescue was a daunting task. With superhuman strength, my handler gently and carefully dug Ethan out of the snowdrift. We bundled him in blankets, warmed him with body heat and emergency supplies, and prepared to return to the base camp for medical assistance. The journey back was slow and deliberate. We moved cautiously, checking for any signs of hypothermia in Ethan. The snow continued to fall, but it no longer seemed as oppressive, a relentless enemy. It was snow now, a landscape we would navigate with newfound resilience and determination.

That night, wrapped in warmth and comfort, I reflected on the ordeal. The city search had been challenging, but this was on another level entirely. It tested our resilience, adaptability, and unbreakable bond. It was a stark reminder of the dangers we face and the steadfast commitment required, highlighting the vital importance of training, preparation, and constant vigilance against nature's unpredictable forces.

The storm had subsided by morning, leaving behind a world transformed by its power. Yet, at the heart of it, there was also a victory. A life saved—a triumph over the elements. The successful rescue became another chapter in our shared journey. A journey that, no matter what the challenges, would always center around the steadfast bond between a human and their devoted canine partner. A bond that extends beyond challenges and rewards, always leading them to the next mission.

CHAPTER 34
The Emotional Toll

The adrenaline rush faded, leaving behind a hollowness that settled deep in my chest. The exhilaration of the rescue, the triumphant feeling of pulling Ethan from the clutches of the blizzard, was quickly replaced by a quiet exhaustion that went beyond the physical. It was a weariness that seeped into my bones, a deep-seated fatigue that touched my soul. My handler, usually so vibrant and full of life, was quiet; a drawn and tired expression had replaced his usual easy smile. He sat beside me, stroking my fur, his hand lingering on my head. The silence between us was thick with unspoken emotions, a shared understanding of the weight we carried.

That night, curled at his feet, I felt a strange disquiet. It was not the familiar post-mission tiredness, the kind that sleep easily erased. This was different; it lingered, a subtle tremor beneath the surface of my calm. I dreamt of the blizzard, Ethan's pale face buried in the snow, and the icy grip of fear that had momentarily clouded my usually sharp senses. The image of his fragile body, his shallow breaths, haunted my dreams, a stark reminder of the fragility of life and the immense responsibility we bear.

The next few days were a blur of routine tasks – training exercises that felt oddly meaningless, meals that held little appeal, and the usual playful interactions that felt strangely hollow. My handler seemed distant, preoccupied, and lost in his thoughts. I noticed the subtle shifts in his demeanor – the slightly strained smile, the way his eyes seemed to drift off into the distance, the more extended silences punctuated by sighs. He was tired, but there was something else, a shadow lurking beneath the surface, something heavier than simple fatigue.

One evening, he sat by the fire, staring into the flames, his face etched with worry lines. He spoke softly, his voice barely a whisper, confiding in me, his canine confidante, about the anxieties that plagued him. He spoke of the what-ifs, the nightmares of what could have happened if they had arrived a few minutes later, if the snow had been deeper, if... the possibilities were endless, each one a chilling reminder of the precarious balance between life and death that they navigated on every mission.

He spoke of the parents, their faces a mix of relief and gratitude as they processed the near-miss, feeling both sorrow and happiness. He described the emotional toll: the fear, anxiety, and lingering trauma they carried. He admitted he was not immune to the weight either, bearing the responsibility for Ethan's life and the knowledge that his actions, or inaction, could mean the difference between life and death.

"It's a strange thing," he said, his voice thick with emotion, "this job. You save a life and are filled with joy and a sense of purpose. But then, the quiet comes, and the weight of it all settles in. It is not physical strain; it is the emotional burden, the knowledge that you have seen the worst, the fragility of life in its rawest form. You carry that with you long after the mission is over." I nudged his hand with my nose, offering silent comfort, my experience echoing his feelings. I understood the weariness and emotional residue these high-stakes missions left behind. The silence between us was a shared language of empathy and understanding, a bond forged not through training but through shared trauma and triumph.

We worked together over the next few weeks to process our shared experiences. He sought professional counseling, a crucial step that he acknowledged as essential. He learned to articulate his emotional reactions and process the emotional fallout of these emotionally charged encounters. He realized that processing these emotions did not diminish his commitment to his job. Instead, it deepened his understanding of the human element of Search and Rescue.

We returned to training, but the atmosphere was different. There was a quiet solemnity and shared understanding that our work was more than physical skill and canine obedience. It was about empathy, understanding the emotional weight of our missions, and acknowledging the importance of self-care and mental resilience.

The following missions were different. The adrenaline was still there, the thrill of the chase, and the satisfaction of a successful rescue. However, they were tempered by a new awareness and a deeper appreciation for the emotional toll. I learned to read his subtle cues, the signs of emotional exhaustion, and to offer him comfort in my way, a gentle nudge, a quiet presence, a warm weight against his leg. He, in turn, became even more attuned to my subtle reactions to shifts in my behavior that indicated stress or emotional fatigue.

He began leaving space in our schedule for simple bonding moments, such as playing fetch in the park, taking long walks on the beach, and quiet evenings curled up together. These moments were crucial, restorative times of peacefulness, a counterbalance to the intensity of our work. We understood that our bond, our mutual support, was the foundation for our success. It was our shield against the emotional toll of our missions, the anchor in the storm.

The emotional toll was real for both of us. It was a complex landscape of exhilaration and exhaustion, triumph and trauma, joy, and sorrow. However, we learned to navigate this landscape together, supporting one another, learning to recognize the signs of stress, and seeking help when needed. We had faced the worst of nature's fury, the fragility of life, and the weight of human suffering. And yet, the bond that connected us, the strength of our partnership, proved to be stronger than any storm. The knowledge we shared in our victory and the toll it took had, in its way, created a stronger, more effective team. It cemented our partnership and our shared commitment to our duty: to seek, to find, to rescue, and to heal. The successful completion of missions was not measured merely by numbers, but by the emotional resilience and stability of the team, ensuring our ability to be ready for the next mission and beyond. Each rescue was a story of skill and determination, shared experience, mutual support, and the unwavering strength of the human-animal bond.

CHAPTER 35

Celebrating Successes, Learning from Setbacks

The scent of pine and damp earth hung heavy in the air as we approached the search area. This time, a lost hiker was reported missing for over 24 hours. The urgency was palpable, the silence broken only by the crunch of leaves under our paws and the rhythmic thump of my handler's heart against his chest, a beat I felt mirroring my own. This mission felt different. The quiet solemnity of our recent reflection had settled into a new rhythm, a deeper understanding of the unspoken language between us. We moved with a calm intensity, our senses heightened, our movements deliberate. My handler's touch was lighter; his commands were softer yet filled with unwavering focus.

We worked as one, a seamless partnership honed by shared experience and mutual trust. The forest floor offered few clues, the wind whispering secrets only the trees could understand. But then, a faint trace, a whisper of scent against the more pungent smells of the woods – a faint musk of sweat, the lingering trace of human presence. My tail throbbed, my body coiled tight with anticipation, my focus laser-sharp on the scent trail. It was faint, almost lost, but I followed it doggedly, my nose to the ground, my handler's quiet encouragement, a steady guide.

The trail led us through tangled undergrowth, fallen logs, and a rushing stream. The terrain was challenging, but my training kicked in – agility and obedience working perfectly. I easily navigated the obstacles; my handler's commands were barely needed as we became one entity. The scent grew stronger and more defined, leading us towards a rocky outcrop. And there, huddled beneath the overhang of a massive rock, shivering and exhausted, was the hiker. Relief washed over me as I saw him, a wave of pure, unadulterated joy that vibrated through my whole being. My handler's voice, filled with emotion, confirmed my find.

The rescue was swift and efficient. My handler reassured the hiker while I stayed close, my presence a comfort against the fear and cold. We brought him to safety, his relief tangible as he was brought to medical attention. The celebratory mood, however, was short-lived. The next search proved more challenging. A young child had wandered off in a busy park, a complex puzzle, his scent easily lost among the myriad other scents. The trail was fragmented, littered with distractions, and the pressure was immense. The initial hours of the search yielded nothing, and the sense of urgency grew with each passing moment. The frustration was palpable, not only for my handler but also for me. I could sense the change in the air and the growing apprehension in his quiet commands.

We searched relentlessly, each missed lead and false scent adding to the challenge. As the sun set, long shadows deepened the sense of desperation. Yet we pressed on. My handler stayed calm, his voice a steady anchor amid the chaos. He encouraged me, adjusted our strategy, and adapted to the shifting conditions. We pushed forward tirelessly, and just as hope began to fade, I found him. Hidden behind a bush, nestled among a pile of discarded toys, the child was asleep. He was safe.

The relief that flooded through me and my handler was overwhelming. It was not the success of the mission but the realization of the importance of our training, our unwavering perseverance, and our mutual trust. We had learned that even the best-laid plans could be confounded by the unpredictable nature of our work and that patience, adaptation, and a tenacious spirit were equally important. The challenges we faced taught us more than any triumph ever could. We learned that setbacks were not failures, but growth opportunities, allowing us to fine-tune our skills and strengthen our bond.

The subsequent missions were a mix of successes and challenges, each adding a new layer to our experience. We learned to adapt to different terrains, navigate complex environments, and interpret increasingly subtle scents. The emotional landscape also deepened. We became more adept at recognizing our limits, at knowing when to pause, when to seek support, and when to appreciate the quiet moments between missions. We learned to process the emotional residue that each search leaves behind. The successes were exhilarating, the failures humbling. But through it all, we learned to rely on each other, grow stronger as a team, and become more resilient and effective.

One challenging mission stands out. A young woman had gone missing in a mountainous region known for its unpredictable weather. The search was difficult, and the terrain was treacherous. The weather shifted dramatically, turning fair weather into a sudden snowstorm. We pressed on, however, fueled by hope and determination. But as night fell, the storm intensified, and the chances of a successful search dimmed. We pressed on. Despite the difficult conditions, we found her injured but alive. We found her huddled under a rocky overhang, her body nearly succumbing to hypothermia. The relief we felt was immeasurable. But the intensity of the experience, the weight of potential failure that loomed over us during the storm, served as a sobering reminder of the risks involved in our work.

It taught us the importance of planning, preparation, and adapting to the unexpected. It underscored the need for constant vigilance and the critical importance of knowing when to call for backup. It also reinforced the importance of teamwork. We worked closely with other search teams, coordinating our efforts, sharing information, and providing mutual support. This experience taught us that, while our bond was crucial, success often relied on collaboration and collective effort. It was a victory achieved by our skills and the team's collective strength.

Whether successful or not, each mission was a lesson in perseverance, adaptability, and the unwavering strength of the human-animal bond. The successes fueled our determination; the failures taught us humility and caution. We learned from each search, honing our skills, refining our techniques, and strengthening our team. We were not searching for missing people; we were searching for ourselves, our limits, and the depth of our partnership. It was a continuous growth journey, a testament to the power of dedication, and a celebration of the extraordinary bond between a dog and his handler.

The quiet moments between missions became as important as the intense moments on the field, allowing for reflection, rest, and strengthening the bond that underpins our success and sustains us through the challenges. Each mission, successful or not, added a new layer of understanding to the bond we share, forging a profound and powerful connection. It reaffirmed our shared commitment to our work.

CHAPTER 36
The Lasting Impact

The years that followed were a blur of adrenaline-fueled searches, quiet moments of reflection, and the unwavering rhythm of our partnership. Each mission, a chapter in our shared story, etched itself onto our souls. The scent of pine needles and damp earth, the chilling dampness of mountain air, and the nervous energy of a frantic family became familiar companions woven into the fabric of our lives.

The faces of those we found, etched with relief and gratitude, became deeply imprinted in my memory. A child's tear-streaked face, the shaky hand of an elderly woman clutching mine, the relieved smile of a mother reunited with her lost son – vivid and profound moments transcended the work itself. They were the heart of it, the reason for our tireless efforts. The echoes resonated long after the final bark had been given, and the last scent trailed.

One particular reunion stands out to me, a vibrant memory that still plays out in my mind's eye. A young girl, no older than seven, had wandered off during a family camping trip. The search area was vast, a dense forest stretching for miles. The days blurred into a harrowing marathon of searching, hope flickering and dying with each passing hour. The frustration was palpable, the weight of responsibility heavy on my handler's shoulders. The scent was faint, almost lost in the complexities of the forest floor, diluted by the wind, rain, and countless other scents. But we persevered, driven by the quiet desperation of the waiting family, their faces mirroring my yearning to find the child. We pressed on, each step, each sniff, a silent prayer. Then, a flash of movement, a fleeting whiff of cotton candy, her favorite scent, among the towering trees. My heart pounded, a frantic drum against my ribs. I raced toward it, my handler's call barely registering as I pushed through the undergrowth. There she was, nestled beneath the roots of an ancient oak, asleep, clutching her worn-out teddy bear. The sheer relief, not only mine but that of the collective family, was overwhelming. It was a moment that transcended the call of duty. It was a moment of pure, unadulterated joy.

The impact of that reunion, of that single moment, extended far beyond that day. I learned later that the little girl, once shy and withdrawn, found newfound courage and resilience. She drew comfort from the thought that she had been found, not by an ordinary dog, but by a dog who had an unwavering loyalty. She started drawing pictures, telling stories about the brave dog that had found her, which helped her confront her fear of being lost in the woods. Her transformation served as a testament to the power of resilience and hope.

The ripple effect of our work spread far wider than the immediate rescues. The stories of our successes inspired countless others, strengthening the bonds between humans and animals. We were not search and rescue dogs; we were symbols of hope, courage, and unwavering loyalty. We inspired many to pursue similar careers and to dedicate their lives to this essential service. Our partnership became a symbol of a collective effort. It became a story celebrating the strength of a bond between a dog and its human, demonstrating that determination and trust could overcome even the most daunting challenges. Beyond the immediate impact on the lives of those we saved, subtler yet equally profound changes occurred in our own lives. The shared experiences of life and death, as well as the shared victories and defeats, forged an unbreakable bond between my handler and me.

The intense focus required during a search sharpened my senses, honed my skills, and fostered deep trust and understanding. He learned the subtle cues of my body language while I anticipated his commands almost before they were uttered. We understood each other on a level beyond words, a silent language of love, loyalty, and shared purpose.

These experiences did not shape our professional lives. They shaped our being. We shared profound moments of both joy and sorrow. We experienced the rush of adrenaline during successful searches and the agonizing wait during difficult ones. We witnessed firsthand the fragility of life and the unwavering strength of the human spirit. These moments, etched deeply into our memories, shaped our personalities, refining our understanding of ourselves and each other. The rigorous training, intense searches, and emotional toll all left their mark. Yet, the rewards outweighed the challenges. The profound satisfaction of knowing we had made a difference, that we had brought hope and healing to families torn apart by loss, was immeasurable. Although gratifying, the recognition paled in comparison to the quiet satisfaction that came with knowing we had served a greater purpose.

Our partnership was not a job; it was a journey. A journey filled with challenges, triumphs, and the kind of profound connection that few ever experience. It was a journey of personal and professional growth, teaching us the importance of resilience, teamwork, and the enduring power of the human-animal bond. This bond, tested and strengthened by every mission, remained the cornerstone of our shared journey. It is a journey I would relive a thousand times over. The lasting impact of our work is not easily measured. It is woven into the fabric of our lives, the lives of those we have helped, and the lives of those whose story we have inspired. It is a testament to the remarkable bond between humans and animals, a celebration of unwavering loyalty, resilience, and the immeasurable power of teamwork. And it is a story that continues to resonate long after the last search is over, a testament to the power of a simple yet profound bond between a dog and his human.

The quiet evenings after a long search, curled up together, the warmth of his hand resting on my head, the shared silence punctuated by the soft rhythm of our breaths—these were the moments that sealed our bond and reaffirmed the profound truth of our partnership. These were not moments of rest; they were moments of connection, rebuilding, and sharing the silent language of understanding that had evolved between us. We had learned to anticipate each other's needs and to offer comfort and support without words.

The years that followed brought their own set of challenges, new searches, new faces, and new stories. But through it all, the core of our partnership remained unchanged. Trust, understanding, and unwavering commitment were the pillars upon which our success was built. We continued to work together, our skills honed, our bond strengthened, and our dedication was unwavering. Our shared journey, marked by the thrill of successful searches and the humility of setbacks, was a powerful testament to the strength of the human-animal bond. It taught us about courage, resilience, and the profound satisfaction that comes from making a difference in the world. It also reinforced the importance of recognizing our limits, knowing when to seek support, and cherishing the quiet moments of connection that bound us together.

And so, the story continues, not in the narrative of our missions but in the quiet moments, the shared glances, and the unwavering trust that binds us together. The legacy of our work extends far beyond the individual searches, touching the lives of those we saved, inspiring others, and serving as a beacon of hope and resilience. The impact is not merely in the number of people found but in the transformation of hearts and strengthening of bonds.

CHAPTER 37

A Legacy of Service

The wind whipped around us, carrying the scent of pine and damp earth —a familiar fragrance that spoke of countless lives found and lost. We stood on the precipice of a new chapter, the sun setting on a decade of service. Retirement loomed, a concept both daunting and liberating. The thought of slowing down, of not having the adrenaline surge of a search, felt strangely unsettling.

Yet, the knowledge that my aging body needed respite was undeniable. My handler, his face lined with the experience of countless missions, stood beside me, his hand resting gently on my flank. We shared a silent understanding, a quiet acknowledgment of our journey together.

It was not about the successful searches, the dramatic reunions that made headlines. It was the countless hours spent training, the endless repetitions of drills, and the unwavering dedication to mastering skills that would one day save a life. The sacrifices, the early mornings, the late nights, the missed family gatherings, all willingly surrendered to the calling. It was the physical toll – the wear and tear on my aging joints, the exhaustion that settled deep in my bones after a long, arduous search. It was the emotional toll, the weight of responsibility, the crushing disappointment of unsuccessful searches, the echoes of lost hopes.

It was not just about the sacrifice, but the deep satisfaction of knowing we had made a difference. It was the joy of seeing relief on reunited families' faces, the gratitude in their eyes, their trembling hands clasped in mine. It was the quiet moments of shared triumph, the unspoken understanding between us, a silent language born of experience and unwavering loyalty.

Our work extended beyond the immediate rescues; it resonated through communities, inspiring hope and fostering trust. We became symbols of courage, resilience, and the unwavering dedication of the human-animal bond. Our story became a testament to what could be achieved when two beings from different worlds worked together, guided by a common purpose. The ripple effect of our actions was far-reaching, inspiring countless others to pursue careers in search and rescue and to dedicate their lives to helping those in need. There was a little boy, I remember, who wrote me a letter filled with childish drawings and heartfelt words of thanks. He had been lost during a hiking trip, separated from his parents in a dense forest. He described the fear, the loneliness, and the overwhelming sense of being lost. Then, he recounted the arrival of a "furry angel," a brave dog who found him and led him back to safety. That letter, framed and displayed on my handler's wall, became a tangible reminder of the impact of our work, a silent testament to the power of our partnership.

Our training had prepared us for the physical demands of search and rescue, but not fully prepared us for the emotional weight. We witnessed scenes of heartbreaking loss, moments of intense human suffering, and the raw grief of families searching for loved ones. These experiences, though challenging, deepened our understanding of the human condition and reinforced our commitment to our work. We learned to manage our emotions and balance the intensity of our work with quiet moments of reflection, which were crucial for our mental and emotional well-being.

We learned, too, the importance of teamwork. Search and rescue weren't about us; it was about the coordinated efforts of countless people – fellow search and rescue teams, police officers, volunteers, and the families of the missing. Each person played a crucial role, contributing their unique skills and expertise to the common goal. The success of our missions depended on this collective effort and the seamless coordination of individuals working towards a common aim. It taught us the power of collaboration, the strength that comes from unity, and the importance of trusting our colleagues.

Retirement was a shift from the adrenaline-fueled urgency of active service to the quiet satisfaction of a life well-lived. We were not leaving search and rescue behind but moving into a new phase of our partnership. Quiet evenings, shared warmth, and gentle companionship became our focus.

The legacy of our service was not the lives we saved, the families we reunited, or the awards we received; it was the lives we saved, the families we reunited, and the awards we received. It was the inspiration we provided, the lives we touched, the hope we instilled. It was the countless others who followed in our footsteps, dedicating their lives to serving their communities and bringing comfort and hope to those in need. It was the quiet affirmation that our efforts had made a tangible difference. It was the enduring power of the human-animal bond, a testament to the incredible capacity for compassion, courage, and unwavering dedication.

This is the legacy of a search and rescue dog. It is a legacy written not in accolades or awards but in the lives touched, the hearts healed, and the enduring strength of a bond that transcends the ordinary. It is a legacy that lives on, not in my memory, but in the hearts and minds of countless others —a testament to the power of service, dedication, and the extraordinary partnership between a human and their dog. This is the story of a life dedicated to service, a legacy woven into the fabric of countless lives. This story lingers long after the final bark has faded. The scent of pine, the feel of damp earth, the weight of responsibility, and the joy of a successful rescue mark a life lived in service, a legacy etched in the hearts of all who knew us.

CHAPTER 38
The Bonds of Friendship

The crisp morning air bit at my nose as I watched Sarah, my handler, interact with the rest of the team. Their laughter, a familiar symphony of camaraderie, echoed across the training grounds. It was not the shared passion for search and rescue that bound them; it was something more profound, a kinship forged in the crucible of shared experiences, of life-or-death situations faced together. They were more than colleagues; they were family.

I had seen it countless times – the quiet moments of support, shared glances of understanding, and unwavering trust between them. After a particularly grueling search, exhausted and emotionally drained, I had witnessed the team huddle together, offering comfort and reassurance, sharing stories and jokes to lighten the burden. They were a network of support, a safety net woven from shared experiences and unwavering loyalty.

Mark was the team leader with unwavering resolve and quiet strength. His leadership was not about issuing orders, but about fostering unity and shared purpose. He possessed an uncanny ability to inspire confidence and motivate his team, even in the face of overwhelming odds. He understood the delicate balance between pushing the team to its limits and ensuring their well-being. He knew when to offer firm encouragement and when a gentle hand on the shoulder was all that was needed.

Then there was Jess, the tracker with keen eyes and an innate ability to read the landscape. She could decipher the subtlest clues, following the faintest of trails with unwavering determination. Her calm demeanor and methodical approach were a calming influence, even in stressful situations. She possessed a deep knowledge of the terrain, and her ability to interpret the subtle signs left behind by a missing person was invaluable. She was the silent anchor of the team, her steady presence a source of comfort and assurance.

David, the medic, was a man of legendary calm and competence. His expertise was crucial, supporting not only the search team but also the families of the missing with comfort and essential first aid. He understood the physical and emotional toll of the work, offering practical support to keep us strong and resilient. His presence was reassuring, his smile a beacon of hope.

Their interactions were not limited to the field. I witnessed their friendships extend beyond the training grounds and rescue missions. They were present at each other's family gatherings, birthdays, and celebrations. They shared an unspoken understanding and a profound respect that went beyond that of professional colleagues. They shared personal struggles and triumphs, offering each other unwavering support and encouragement.

I remember one particular Christmas gathering. The team had gathered at Mark's house, the air filled with the aroma of roasting turkey and festive cheer. Children ran around, their laughter mingling with the cheerful chatter of adults. It was not a joyous occasion, but a testament to their enduring friendship. They were more than colleagues; they were a family united by their shared commitment to search and rescue, as well as enduring friendships.

The bonds they shared were not forged in a day; they were years in the making, built on shared experiences, mutual respect, and a profound understanding of each other's strengths and weaknesses. They learned to trust each other implicitly, to rely on each other in times of crisis, and to celebrate each other's successes. Their camaraderie was more than a comfortable working atmosphere; it was the foundation of their effectiveness. The glue held them together, enabling them to function as a cohesive unit capable of overcoming any obstacle.

Their teamwork was something to behold, a seamless symphony of coordinated effort. Each member knew their role, their strengths, and limitations. They could anticipate each other's needs, reacting instinctively to the evolving circumstances. Their shared experiences created an unspoken understanding, enabling them to work seamlessly and efficiently.

Their friendships were not merely about companionship; they were a vital component of their success. They provided emotional support, offering comfort and reassurance during stressful moments and celebrating the triumphs together. The strength of their friendships bolstered their resilience, empowering them to cope with the emotional toll of their demanding work.

The success of our missions was not solely due to our training or our skills; it was also a testament to the power of our teamwork and unshakeable bond. Their camaraderie created a safe and supportive environment, allowing each member to perform at their best, even under immense pressure. They were a force to be reckoned with, a team whose collective strength was far greater than the sum of their abilities.

Their bond was a testament to the human spirit, the capacity for compassion, and resilience in the face of adversity. They inspired me and constantly reminded me of the power of teamwork and the enduring strength of human connection. Their example taught me the value of companionship, mutual support, and the unwavering loyalty that characterizes true friendship. Their friendship was a powerful force, a beacon of hope in the often-dark world of search and rescue.

The years spent working alongside them weren't about the successful rescues or the moments of shared triumph. They were about the quiet moments of camaraderie, the shared laughter, the unspoken understanding that passed between us. They were about the enduring friendships forged in the crucible of shared experiences, the bonds that had grown stronger with each passing mission, and the unwavering support that had sustained us through times of adversity.

These were the true treasures of my career, the memories I cherished most. They were the unsung heroes, the silent guardians, the unwavering pillars of support who made our work not only possible but meaningful. And in their steadfast companionship, I found a loyalty and a love that mirrored my bond with my human.

And as the sun set on my career, it was these friendships, these shared experiences, and these unwavering bonds that I would cherish most —the echoes of laughter and camaraderie resonating long after the final search had ended.

CHAPTER 39
A Life Well Lived

The scent of pine and damp earth filled my nostrils, a familiar comfort after years spent scouring forests and mountainsides. The sun, low in the western sky, cast long shadows across the familiar training grounds, painting the landscape in hues of orange and purple. It was a peaceful scene, starkly contrasting with the urgency and intensity of the countless searches I had undertaken. But as I lay here, the familiar ache in my aging joints was a constant companion, and profound contentment washed over me.

My life had not been a simple tale of chasing squirrels and napping in sunbeams. It had been a tapestry woven with threads of intense training, exhilarating rescues, and the unwavering companionship of my human, Sarah. We had faced challenges that tested our limits and moments that pushed us to the brink of exhaustion and despair. Yet, through it all, our bond had only grown more substantial as a testament to the enduring power of the connection between a dog and its human.

I recall the first time I caught the scent of a missing person, the frantic energy of their scent clinging to the undergrowth. It was a jarring sensation, a sharp contrast to the playful energy I had been accustomed to. The seriousness of the mission, the weight of responsibility, settled heavily upon me. It was a moment that altered my perspective, shifting my focus from playful games to the profound significance of my role. From that day forward, the scent of fear became a clarion call, a driving force that propelled me forward, guiding my steps with unwavering determination.

The years that followed were a blur of intense training, grueling exercises, and countless hours spent honing my skills. The agility courses, initially daunting obstacles, became familiar pathways; my paws moved with practiced ease across the uneven terrain. Initially frustrating and confusing, the scent work became second nature, my nose guiding me through the intricate maze of scents that whispered stories of the missing. The countless hours spent practicing obedience were not exercises in discipline; they were building blocks for the unwavering focus and precision crucial in the critical moments of a search.

Each successful mission was a victory, not just for me, but for the entire team and for the families whose hope had been rekindled by our efforts. The relief etched on the faces of reunited families was a reward more valuable than any treat. Their tears of joy and heartfelt gratitude—these were the moments that cemented the profound significance of my work, the understanding that I was more than a dog; I was a crucial part of a team dedicated to bringing people home.

However, there were also heart-wrenching moments, as the stark reality of searches that ended without success was evident. The lingering scent of desperation, the silence that hung heavy in the air—these moments etched themselves into my memory, reminding me of our immense responsibility. These were the times when my team's support and Sarah's quiet strength became a lifeline, bolstering my spirits and guiding me through the depths of my sadness.

The emotional weight of these searches was often heavier on Sarah than on me. I saw the toll it took on her – the sleepless nights, the anxious pacing, the exhaustion that etched itself into her face. Yet, she always managed to find the strength to continue and persevere, driven by an unwavering commitment to our shared mission. Her steadfast faith in me, her quiet words of encouragement, her gentle touch – these were the anchors that kept me steady during the darkest moments.

Sarah, my human, was more than my handler; she was my partner, my friend, and my family. Our bond transcended the conventional relationship between a dog and its owner. We understood each other without words, communicating through subtle cues, shared glances, and an unspoken language of mutual trust and affection. She sensed my anxieties, fears, and triumphs. I felt her emotions, her joy, her sorrow, her determination. Our connection was a powerful force, a silent symphony of shared experiences, unwavering loyalty, and unbreakable affection.

My work was not about finding missing persons; it was about offering hope, reassurance, and comfort to their loved ones. The simple act of sniffing out a lost child, of guiding my human to a missing hiker, was often more than a rescue; it was an act of healing, a calming to the despair of families caught in the throes of fear and uncertainty. The quiet dignity of a successful mission, the shared relief of the team, the heartfelt gratitude of the families – these moments were etched into the fabric of my being, a testament to the power of teamwork, the importance of dedication, and the enduring strength of the human spirit.

And now, as I look back on my life, I see not a series of individual events but a rich and fulfilling narrative. A life dedicated to service, helping others, and making a difference. A life filled with challenges, triumphs, and the unwavering companionship of my human. A life lived to the fullest, leaving an indelible mark on the hearts of those I have encountered. My story is not my own; it is a testament to the powerful bond between humans and animals, a celebration of loyalty, courage, and the unwavering dedication of a team united by a shared purpose.

The setting sun cast a warm glow on my aging face, a comforting reminder of the warmth and affection that had filled my life. Sarah's soft padding on my head was a familiar comfort, a silent acknowledgment of the journey we had shared. The years had passed quickly, a blur of activity and purpose, yet the memories remained sharp and vibrant, each a testament to my life and the difference I had made.

It was not the successful rescues that defined my life; it was the quiet moments of camaraderie, the shared laughter, the unspoken understanding that existed between us. It was the enduring friendships forged in the crucible of shared experiences, the bonds that had grown stronger with each passing mission, and the unwavering support that had sustained us through times of adversity. These were the true treasures of my career, the memories I cherished most. These were the unsung heroes, the silent guardians, the unwavering pillars of support who made our work not only possible but meaningful.

The scent of woodsmoke and damp earth still stirred within me, a comforting reminder of the countless hours spent in the heart of the wilderness, searching for those lost and in need. The feel of the wind in my fur, the sun on my back, the exhilarating rush of a successful search – the sensations that defined my existence, the essence of my being.

Reflecting on my years of service, the scent of pine and damp earth still fresh in my memory, I find myself embarking on a new chapter of my life: retirement.

The setting sun, now a comforting reminder of the warmth and fulfillment that comes with my career, also signals the close of my active days. While my body may slow, my spirit remains eager, and I find a purpose in assisting my handler, Sarah, in training a new partner. The role of the mentor is a rewarding one. I take pride in passing on my knowledge and skills to the next generation, ensuring the continuity of our vital work. With each new challenge, I feel the excitement and urgency of my younger days' return. I demonstrate the intricate art of scent work, guiding the eager pupil through the maze of aromas, imparting the wisdom gained from countless searches.

Together, we navigate agility courses, my experienced paws guiding their tentative steps, building their confidence with each obstacle conquered. In this new phase, I also get to savor the quiet moments of companionship with Sarah, free from the weight of our former responsibilities. We stroll through the familiar training grounds, the sun warming our faces as we share a silent understanding of the impact we have had. The memories of our shared adventures remain sharp, and I know that the bond we forged will endure, even as new partnerships form.

CHAPTER 40

The Enduring Power of the Human-Animal Bond

The quiet rustle of leaves underfoot, the scent of pine needles sharp in the air – these were the familiar comforts of the forest, where Sarah and I had spent countless hours searching, hoping, finding. The memories, like fragments of a dream, flooded back: the frantic energy of a missing child's scent, the unwavering determination in Sarah's eyes, the overwhelming joy of a successful reunion. These were the moments that defined us and cemented our bond, a bond that transcended the simple relationship between a dog and its handler. It was a partnership forged in shared purpose, strengthened by mutual respect, and cemented by an unbreakable love.

Our work was not always easy. There were times when the scent grew cold, hope seemed to dwindle, and the weight of responsibility pressed heavily on our shoulders. Some searches ended in heartbreak, the silence of the woods echoing the emptiness in our hearts. These were the times when our bond was truly tested, and the unwavering support of our team, along with Sarah's quiet strength, became our lifeline. In these moments of despair, the actual depth of our connection was revealed. We found solace in each other's company. Sarah's hands, calloused from years of hard work, held mine gently, a familiar comfort in the moments of exhaustion and despair. Her quiet words of encouragement, gentle touch, and unwavering faith in me were the anchors that kept me steady during the storm, the quiet assurances that helped me navigate the darkness. She understood the emotional weight I carried, the silent burden of responsibility. She saw the toll it took, not on my body but on my spirit. And in her unwavering love and support, I found the strength to continue, persevere, and remain faithful to my purpose.

Our bond was more than a partnership; it was a testament to the extraordinary capacity for love and loyalty between humans and animals. It was a connection that transcended words, a silent symphony of shared experiences, unspoken understanding, and unwavering affection. We communicated not through barks and commands but through subtle cues. We shared glances—a silent language born of years spent working side by side, trusting implicitly in each other's abilities.

It was not the successful rescues that forged our bond; it was the moments of quiet contemplation, the laughter we shared during lighter times, and the unwavering support we offered in moments of difficulty. It was the quiet companionship, unspoken understanding, and steadfast loyalty. The shared meals in the field, the peaceful evenings by the campfire, and the unspoken bond that developed between us through hardship and joy transcended the conventional handler-dog relationship. It evolved into a friendship, a partnership, and a family.

The faces of the families we reunited, the overwhelming relief, the tears of joy, the heartfelt gratitude—these were the rewards that fueled our dedication, the moments that made our work worthwhile. To witness the reuniting of a lost child with their frantic parents, to see the relief flood their faces as they were led back to safety – these were the moments that cemented the significance of our work and deepened the emotional connection we shared. The sheer joy of those moments reverberated throughout our being, reinforcing the sense of purpose and dedication that drove us.

Our work extended beyond the physical act of searching. It was about offering hope, providing comfort, and instilling reassurance. The simple act of locating a lost hiker, which often led Sarah to a missing child, became more than a rescue; it was an act of healing, a calming to the despair of families in their most vulnerable moments. The quiet dignity of a successful mission, the shared relief of our team, and the collective satisfaction were the defining elements of our success, not in finding the missing person but also in restoring hope and offering support to those who needed it most.

Looking back, I realize that our journey was not a series of individual missions but a narrative of shared experiences, unwavering loyalty, and unbreakable bonds. It was a testament to the enduring power of the human-animal connection and the extraordinary capacity for love, service, and selfless dedication. It was a story of shared triumph and sorrow, a tale of partnership and unwavering support, told in the language of scent, touch, and shared glances.

The years that followed were a blur of activity, a whirlwind of training, searches, and reunions. Each successful mission was a victory, not just for me, but for the entire team —a testament to our collective effort and dedication. The trust between Sarah and me was absolute; our partnership had matured into a symphony of unspoken understanding, a perfect harmony of human intuition and canine senses.

But even the most successful partnerships face challenges. At times, fatigue threatened to overwhelm us when the emotional toll of unsuccessful searches weighed heavily on our hearts. There were times when the scent grew cold, hope dwindled, and the weight of our responsibility pressed down, threatening to crush us under its burden. In these difficult moments, the true strength of our bond was put to the test, and the depth of our connection was revealed.

We learned to rely on one another, to support each other, and to find solace in each other's company. Sarah's quiet strength and her unwavering belief in me became my anchor in the storm. My steadfast loyalty and dedication to our shared mission gave her the strength to persevere and to face the challenges with renewed determination. We shared not only our successes but also our failures, disappointments, hopes, and dreams. Our connection deepened with each day, strengthening with every challenge we overcame.

The final sunset cast a warm glow on our shared memories, a gentle reminder of our life, our bond, and the difference we made. It was not the successful rescues, but the quiet moments of shared companionship, the laughter, the unspoken understanding, and the steadfast loyalty, that were the veritable treasures — the lasting legacies of our partnership. They were the unsung heroes of our story, the silent guardians, the unwavering pillars of support that made our work not only possible but meaningful.

The years of tireless service eventually took their toll, and the thought of retirement loomed. It was a tough decision, but one that I knew was necessary. My body, once tireless in its pursuit, now carried the weight of our endeavors, and I knew it was time to pass the torch. A new partner, eager and full of potential, awaited their turn, and I was honored to become a mentor. Passing my knowledge and skills to the next generation was rewarding. I witnessed the same unwavering determination in this new partner that I had seen in Sarah, and it filled me with pride and hope. Together, we embarked on a new journey, one where I guided them through the intricacies of our work, sharing the lessons I had learned over the years. The mentor role suited me, and I found joy in supporting and guiding those following in my footsteps. It was a unique bond, one forged on respect and a shared goal of making a difference. I knew the skills I imparted would help them forge their paths and create stories of triumph and sorrow. It was a new chapter that allowed me to reflect on the impact of our work and the legacy we left behind. The quiet rustle of leaves underfoot during our training walks reminded me of the countless hours Sarah and I had spent in these woods. With the new partner by my side, I felt peace knowing that the work we started would continue through the next generation.

Acknowledgments

Foremost, I am grateful to all the Search and Rescue K9 Handlers and Instructors who inspired this narrative. Your constant passion and dedication to these amazing Search and Rescue K9s never cease to fill me with both wonder and admiration. Future Search and Rescue K9 Handlers, who dream of establishing careers working with talented dogs, deserve special recognition for the vibrant story this brings to life. The creative vision uniquely and captivatingly shaped the narrative, thus providing an extra layer of depth to the story.

To my family, whose unwavering support and encouragement made this book possible. Thank you for believing in my dreams and sharing in the journey. Your love and faith have been my guiding light, and I am forever grateful for your presence. You have been my rock, my cheerleader, and my inspiration. This book is as much yours as it is mine.

I'd also like to thank my illustrator, Karen Shayler, and my editor, Roxana Coumans, for their indispensable help and support during the book's publication. This story wouldn't be alive without your keen eye, insightful feedback, and endless patience. This project has benefited from your dedication to excellence and belief in its success.

I am deeply grateful for the invaluable guidance of my reviewers, especially my mother, Billie Aylesworth of Diamond B Cutting Horses, and Dr. Jennifer Boucher of Diamond J Veterinary Services. Your feedback has brought authenticity and depth to this story, and your love for animals and commitment to excellence continue to inspire me.

We sincerely thank every reader who has joined us on this journey. This book exists because of your love for stories and your belief in the magic of friendship and perseverance. We hope this narrative inspires you to pursue your dreams, nurture your friendships, and cherish the relationships that enrich your life.

Author Biography

Author Brett Shayler, a lifelong horse enthusiast and dedicated Search and Rescue volunteer, has always drawn inspiration from his K9 partners, including his current retired Alex and former partners Tara, Dewey, and Quendi.

The story is told from the perspective of a search dog, and I hope readers will see the influence of the unique insights my K9 partners have shared with me over the years.

I am deeply grateful for the kindness, loyalty, and love each of these dogs shared, teaching invaluable lessons along the way. Growing up on a ranch surrounded by animals, Shayler brings to his stories a vivid portrayal of the deep, enduring bonds between people and the animals they care for throughout their lives.

Drawing inspiration from his family's vast acreage and the wild horses that roam freely upon it, Brett lovingly crafts heartwarming tales that not only celebrate the bonds of friendship but also extol the virtues of a deep respect for the natural world and the remarkable connections that exist in the relationships between people and animals. Through his books, he hopes to cultivate curiosity, compassion, and a thirst for knowledge in young readers. Brett often escapes to nature, hiking and observing wildlife, finding inspiration for his writing away from his desk.

www.ingramcontent.com/pod-product-compliance
Lightning Source LLC
Chambersburg PA
CBHW030344030726
47499CB00003B/887